S0-AAE-885

Falling For The Wrong Hustla 2

Tina J

DOUGLASS BRANCH LIBRARY
Champaign Public Library
504 East Grove Street
Champaign, Illinois 61820-3239

Copyright 2019

This novel is a work of fiction. Any resemblances to actual events, real people, living or dead, organizations, establishments or locales are products of the author's imagination. Other names, characters, places, and incidents are used fictionally.

All parts reserved. No part of this book may be used or reproduced in any form or by any means electronic or mechanical, including photocopying, recording or by information storage and retrieval system, without written permission from the publisher and write.

Because of the dynamic nature of the Internet, any web address or links contained in this book may have changed since publication, and may no longer be valid.

Warning:

This book is strictly Urban Fiction and the story is **NOT**

REAL!

Characters will not behave the way you want them to; nor will

they react to situations the way you think they should. Some of

them may be drug addicts, kingpins, savages, thugs, rich, poor,

ho's, sluts, haters, bitter ex-girlfriends or boyfriends, people

from the past and the list can go on and on. That is what Urban

Fiction mostly consists of. If this isn't anything you foresee

yourself interested in, then do yourself a favor and don't read it

because it's only going to piss you off. ☺☺

Also, the book will not end the way you want so please be

advised that the outcome will be based solely on my own

thoughts and ideas. I hope you enjoy this book that y'all made

me write. Thanks so much to my readers, supporters, publisher

and fellow authors and authoress for the support. ☺☺

Author Tina J

More books from me:

The Thug I Chose 1, 2 & 3

A Thin Line Between Me and My Thug 1 & 2

I Got Luv For My Shawty 1 & 2

Kharis and Caleb: A Different Kind of Love 1 & 2

Loving You Is A Battle 1 & 2 & 3

Violet and The Connect 1 & 2 & 3

You Complete Me

Love Will Lead You Back

This Thing Called Love

Are We In This Together 1,2 &3

Shawty Down To Ride For a Boss 1, 2 &3

When A Boss Falls in Love 1, 2 & 3

Let Me Be The One 1 & 2

We Got That Forever Love

Aint No Savage Like The One I Got 1&2

A Queen and A Hustla 1, 2 & 3

Thirsty For A Bad Boy 1&2

Hassan and Serena: An Unforgettable Love 1&2

Caught Up Loving A Beast 1, 2 & 3

A Street King And His Shawty 1 & 2

I Fell For The Wrong Bad Boy 1&2

I Wanna Love You 1 & 2

Addicted to Loving a Boss 1, 2, & 3

I Need That Gangsta Love 1&2

Creepin With The Plug 1 & 2

All Eyes On The Crown 1,2&3

When She's Bad, I'm Badder: Jiao and Dreek, A Crazy

Love Story 1,2&3

Still Luvin A Beast 1&2

Her Man, His Savage 1 & 2

Marco & Rakia: Not Your Ordinary, Hood Kinda Love 1,2

& 3

Feenin For A Real One 1, 2 & 3

A Kingpin's Dynasty 1, 2 & 3

What Kinda Love Is This: Captivating A Boss 1, 2 & 3

Frankie & Lexi: Luvin A Young Beast 1, 2 & 3

A Dope Boys Seduction 1, 2 & 3

My Brother's Keeper 1. 2 & 3

C'Yani & Meek: A Dangerous Hood Love 1, 2 & 3

When A Savage Falls for A Good Girl 1, 2 & 3

Eva & Deray 1 & 2

Blame It On His Gangsta Luv 1 & 2

Remi

"Its not fair Remi. I've been fucking with you a lot longer. How you find a new bitch to claim?" Monee whined. She had been texting me nonstop and I avoided her at all costs. Most women take the hint when a nigga don't return their call but not her.

The only reason I'm talking to her now is because she caught me coming in Club Turquoise. Its closed for the grand opening of my new spot but I had to grab some papers from here. The bitch must've been waiting here all day.

"First off… don't call her a bitch and second… I've never told you I'd be your man." I grabbed what I needed and shut my office door.

"Let's go." I had her wait downstairs because she ain't my girl and no one comes in my office anyway except Cat.

"REMIIIIIIII!" She whined following me to the back door.

"Wait!" I opened the side door and turned around.

"What?"

"Let me make you feel good real quick." Something was suspect as fuck with Monee. If I tell her I'm out she doesn't chase after me or maybe she does and I leave in such a hurry, I pay it no mind.

"Back the fuck up." She pushed me against the wall and tried her hardest to get my jeans down. When she didn't succeed, her hands went under my shirt. She kissed my stomach and I pushed her off. It sounds like I let her but trust a nigga moved her the fuck back.

"Hold up! You smell that?"

"I don't smell nothing. I wanna fuck Remi." I moved past her and let my senses lead me to the smell. I walked in the kitchen and there was a small fire on the stove. I grabbed the fire extinguisher and put it out. Who the fuck was here? I couldn't help but think about Cat mentioning Ivan tryna sabotage my spots.

"Who tryna set your shit on fire?" Monee questioned as she fanned her face.

"I don't know. Let's go." She followed behind me without tryna fuck which made me stop.

"Oh you don't wanna fuck no more?" I asked to hear her response.

"Fuck it. You said no." *BINGO!* Something wasn't right. I didn't have the time to bother with the shit and locked up.

I called Tara up and had her come to the club with a fire inspector to check it out. I wanted the security footage sent to my phone and told her we'll link up at the opening. I sat in my car and watched Monee hop on her phone immediately. I just shook my head because it meant she was tryna set me up, but why? I drove to my house with many thoughts on my mind. I'll have to deal with it tomorrow.

****

"Mmmm, don't stop Remi." Naima moaned out as I hit it from the back.

"You like this dick Naima?"

"I love it. Oh shit. Oh shit." Her body shook as the orgasm took over. She fell flat on the bed. I turned her over and reentered my new favorite spot.

"Remi we're gonna be late."

"Its my place. We can be fashionably late." She used her arm to push me off.

"In that case, let me go for a ride." I smiled, laid on the bed and placed my hands behind my head.

"Got damn you feel good as fuck." I told her. We finished fucking the shit outta each other, hopped in the shower and got dressed.

"If I don't say it later, I'm proud of you Remi." She looked up at me with those innocent eyes.

"Thank you."

"I mean it. In the short time we've known one another you worked your ass off, and I admire you for it. One day I'm gonna have my own business and I hope I'm as successful as you." I pulled her close.

"I'm glad you're by my side. Besides my mom and pops, there's no one else I'd want there."

"Awww baby."

"And you'll be successful at anything you do." We started kissing again and she moved away.

"You know a kiss lands us right back in the bed. Let's go."

"Maybe you should stop kissing me." I said following her down the steps.

"I love seeing your dick get hard. Your reaction, gives me one and the consequence is always good." I smacked her on the ass.

"Let's see how good it is when we get home later. You wanted it rough earlier and we were on a time limit but make no mistake Naima. I'm gonna give it to you."

"I can't wait." We left the house and arrived hand in hand on the red carpet I had out. Like all places who have grand openings, I had the newspapers, local news and radio station personalities there.

"Baby I'm gonna use the bathroom. Go mingle with your guest but don't get fucked up." I laughed. Naima disappeared in the crowd. I walked around speaking to

12

everyone and making sure the bartenders kept people's drinks filled.

"Congratulations son." I turned around and my pops was standing there in a suit.

"How the hell did you get here?" We embraced one another and for the first time we didn't have to stop. The CO's usually give us a hard time. Not that we wanna hug long but they don't even give you a second to do it.

"I wanted to surprise you. Cat picked me up earlier and I stayed at his place." I figured that because Cat only stayed in his own place if him and Ivy were arguing.

"Where is he? Him and Ivy were supposed to walk in with us." I glanced around and didn't see them anywhere.

"I'm not sure but how I look?" He did a turn in his suit.

"Good pops. Did mom see you yet?" I think so. He pointed and my mother stood there with tears in her eyes. I had to walk over and lead her to where my father was because her feet must've been stuck. The two of them hugged and wouldn't let go. I thought about letting them go in my office but its been a long time and my pops will probably wanna fuck all night. Plus, only me and my girl fucking in there anyway.

"Good job bro." Ivan said and patted my back. I had no idea he was coming because I hadn't heard from him after I beat his ass and he wasn't invited.

"Thanks." I went to walk away and he said something to make me turn around.

"How you think Naima would feel knowing you were with Monee earlier?" I snatched him up by his shirt.

"What the fuck you say?"

"You heard me. I stopped by Club Turquoise to apologize to you and Monee had you hemmed up against the wall. She must have some good pussy if you risking your so called new love interest."

"I didn't fuck or touch that bitch."

"Son let him go. Hello Ivan." Its like my brother saw a ghost. His eyes got big as hell.

"You may not have fucked her but she took it as an open invitation to come." He pointed to a woman who had the same shape as Monee, but it couldn't be her. I didn't invite that bitch here.

"Pops." Ivan spoke and walked away.

"What's going on?"

"I think Ivan set me up to try and fuck Monee and get this." I ran my hand over my face.

"There was a small kitchen fire in Club Turquoise. Had I not been there it would've grown. I think he did it."

"Get him the fuck outta here before he does something else." Me and my pops walked around looking for him.

"Hey babe." I heard Naima behind me.

"Hey. Have you seen my brother?" Her face turned up.

"Stay close. He's here and I don't want him bothering you." She nodded and intertwined her hand in mine. I was about to introduce her to my father until one of my workers interrupted.

"Boss, we need some more liquor and Tara isn't here yet." I'm the only other person with the key to the cellar where the liquor is. I didn't trust anyone.

"I'll get it Remi." Naima had her hand out for the keys. I was reluctant to give them to her.

"Its ok."

"Remi this is your big night. Stay here with your guests. I'll be right back." I was struggling with letting her outta my sight.

"Watch her." I told one of the bouncers. He followed behind Naima and the worker. I picked my phone up to call Cat and he didn't answer. Where the fuck is he?

"Have you seen Cat and Ivy?" My mom asked. Her and Ivy's mom were together drinking like always.

"Nah. I just called and he didn't answer. Something don't feel right." I told them and both of their facial expressions changed.

"We're gonna go by the house because its not like them to miss anything this big." His mom said and they both gave me a hug.

"Ok and call me as soon as you get there." When they left, I went to find my brother.

16

"Damn Remi, this is nice." The nightmare I got rid of earlier stood in my face. She looked good but she's not my cup of tea anymore.

"Move the fuck on."

"Why? You don't want your girl to see us?"

"Bitch get the fuck out." I left her standing there and went in search of Naima. She was taking too long to come back. I noticed her talking to Tara and she didn't look happy. I hope Monee didn't say shit to her.

Naima

"Ok, I think we have enough for you to finish the night without having to return." I told the chick Sandy. She's the employee who asked Remi to get more liquor.

"I hope so. These people hear free drinks and you'd swear they were tryna drink for the rest of their lives." We both laughed.

"Let me lock up and I'll be right behind you." She stood off to the side and I told the bouncer he could go upstairs to check on everything. I didn't want him gone too long and Remi get mad.

"Can I help you? No one is supposed to be down here?" Sandy asked someone coming down the steps. I locked the door and turned to see Remi's ignorant ass brother.

"Ms. Carter and I know one another, and my brother don't care if I come down here." Sandy didn't know what to say.

"We're ok Sandy. Let Mr. Stevens know we should be good for the night." I told her she could go. I wasn't about to portray how nervous he made me.

"What can I do for you Ivan, or Mr. Stevens?" I stood there with my arms folded.

"Let me be the first to say, you are stunning in this dress." He walked around me licking his lips.

"You're nowhere near the first person to say it but thanks." I gave him a fake smile.

"I'm sure."

"Anyway, I wanted to apologize for the way we met. I was wrong and a man should never treat a woman that way. I also apologize for watching you at my brother's house." He licked his lips like the creep he is. *So he was watching me.*

"Its ok. Is that all?" I went to walk past him, and he grabbed my wrist.

"My brother seems to be in love with you, which is weird because he's never felt this way about any woman." My heart fluttered when he mentioned Remi loving me. I was nervous giving him my heart but to hear him verify it only made me happier.

"I'm glad he feels the same as I." I took a step forward and he stopped me again.

"You know, I think its lust because if it were love he'd never cheat on you." He now had my full attention.

"Excuse me."

"Yea earlier I was at Club Turquoise waiting for him and the other chick he fucks with was there and they looked very cozy."

"Yea right." He smirked.

"I knew I'd see you here and you wouldn't believe me, so I recorded it." He pulled his phone out.

"I swear these phone companies hit the lottery when they came out with this shit." He passed me the phone and sure enough there Remi stood with a woman in front of him. Her hands were under his shirt as he stared down at her. I pushed the phone back in his hand when she reached for Remi's jeans. I couldn't watch anymore.

"I told you." One single tear fell down my face and he took it as me being vulnerable. He reached out and hugged me. I struggled tryna get him off, pushed him back and ran up the steps.

"What's wrong? You ok?" Tara asked. She was at the top.

"I'm fine. Can I use your car to go?"

"Go? Why are you leaving?" She peeked around me and frowned her face up. She must've saw Ivan.

"Hey cuz!" Ivan moved past me and squeezed my ass. I smacked the shit outta him and he yoked me up.

"You obviously don't remember the last time." My feet were dangling as he continued choking me.

"Ivan get the fuck off her. What are you doing?" Tara was punching him in the back.

"YOOOO!" I saw Remi hit his brother and it knocked him out. Ivan's body hit the ground hard as hell. Luckily, the area we were in no one could see because I'm sure his guests would have a field day with this.

"You ok? What happened?" Remi was checking me over. I saw hands wrap around his waist.

"Baby, what's going on over here?"

"Baby?" I questioned and looked at the woman. I didn't have to say a word to know she's the one he was with earlier.

"Bitch you crazy?" Remi pushed her off.

"You weren't saying that earlier."

"What?" Remi turned around with the evilest look I've ever seen on him. It was worse than the one at the hospital.

"No need to deny it Remi. I saw the video. Tara can I have your keys please? I promise not to crash your car."

"You're not leaving Naima. She's lying." Remi tried pleading with me, but I saw the video.

"Is she? I mean that wasn't her who ran her hands under your shirt?" He didn't say a word.

"She wasn't tryna get your pants down at the restaurant earlier? Is that why you wanted to have sex before we came? Were you thinking about her?" Tara covered her mouth.

"You know what? It doesn't even matter. Why would I think a man who's never been in love could be faithful?

Goodbye Remi." I ran out the building and saw my mother pulling up. She never met Remi and I thought tonight would be perfect. I told her not to get out and I was leaving with her.

"What's going on here?" I heard before getting in the car. Some man stood there looking like an exact replica of Remi.

"Remington?" My mother spoke out the window in a confused tone.

"Remington who?" I questioned my mother because she couldn't be talking about the person I think she is.

"Nyeemah?" He asked the same thing and confused as well.

"Ma, please don't say this is who I think it is." My mother got out the car and walked over to him. Remi, his mom, Tara and another woman was standing there.

"Nyeemah?" Now his mother asked the same thing. Its like they couldn't believe their eyes.

"Its exactly who he is Naima. Here in the flesh. But how?" My mom didn't appear to be as upset as I thought she should be.

"No. No. No. No. It can't be." I walked over to where she was.

"Did you know Remi? Is that why you showed interest? You felt bad for me." I asked with tears falling down my face.

"Did I know what? What the fuck is going on?" Remi asked and no one said a word. His parents still seemed to be shocked at my mom showing up.

"How could you do me like that Remi? I loved you, I'm in love with you and this is how you repay me by keeping your father a secret."

"A secret? My father ain't no secret. You know all about him. I told you everything." I chuckled.

"Everything but the truth."

"The truth?"

"Yes, Remi the truth." He came closer to me.

"Naima, I admit the shit at the other club is suspect as fuck, but I can explain. As far as my father, there's nothing I didn't tell you about him."

"Oh, so you know he's the man who killed my father?"

24

Mario

"Her mom left so you're gonna have a few hours at the most." The guy said. Tonight, they had me going to retrieve whatever item it is from Naima's mother's house.

"Where's the stuff?" I asked referring to the sledgehammer and shit he said I needed to get behind the wall.

"Everything is on the side of her house in bushes."

"A'ight, I'm going now." I disconnected the call, ran down the steps and hopped in my car. I was finally healed after that nigga beat my ass at the gym. I ain't even mad because I was being petty.

I didn't know Naima moved on and hearing she did pissed me off. I also didn't expect the nigga to almost kill me either. I barely got one punch in. At least I know he'll protect her.

"WAIT!" Lina screamed out and ran to my car. She tried to get in and I kept the door locked.

"I'm coming too."

"Go back in the house Lina. Who the fuck gonna watch the kids?" She thought about what I said and backed away.

I pulled off thinking about how this is almost over. I can give Naima her house back, get rid of Lina and move on with my life. Its been nothing but a bunch of bullshit since Lina's been in my life and if I didn't know any better, I'd say she set all of it up. I know she ran her mouth about Naima, but she knows too much and been acting funny lately.

I drove past Ivy's house on the way and noticed mad cops, ambulances and coroners. I wonder what the fuck happened over there. I kept going until I reached Naima's mom house, parked down the street and prepared myself to be a damn demolition man. I still don't understand why these people couldn't do it. If they had that much power, they could've gone inside, tied her mom up and took it.

"Shit." I said to myself when I tripped over the curb. Hell yea I'm nervous. It may be dark out, but people are nosy.

I found the bag in the bushes and lifted the rug for the extra key. I only know its there because her mom stayed losing her keys. Naima told her to get one of those key boxes instead of putting it under the rug. I guess she didn't listen because here I am, entering the same spot my ex girl used to live in before getting her house.

I closed the door and made my way up the steps. It was a three-bedroom house and I had no idea which room he was talking about. I couldn't call back because the man always called from an unknown number. The only information they did give me is the spot is close to the closet. Each room only had one so it shouldn't be too bad. I took the sledgehammer out and started the process.

BOOM! BOOM! Each time I swung, the shit was loud as hell. I prayed no one heard me and called the cops.

The first room had nothing in it, neither did the second, which was the master bedroom. I went in the last one that held Naima's old room and smiled at the photos on her dresser. A few of them were of me and her.

When she moved out, she didn't take anything, and her mother must've left the room alone. I reminisced for a second about all the good times we used to have. My phone ringing brought me out my zone.

"Hello."

"Did you get it?" Lina asked.

Why you calling me?"

"Hurry up Mario. I don't want you to get caught."

"If you hang up, I can get back to it."

"Mario if she has new stuff bring it to me. I wore everything here already." I hung the phone up on her dumb ass. Hopefully, they take her out when I get whatever this is.

I swung the sledgehammer and the wall didn't break. In the other rooms it wasn't a problem, which led me to believe this is the spot. I broke the wall around it and ten minutes later a big black safe appeared.

"Well I'll be damned." I slid it out slowly and placed it on the bed. I pulled on the handle thinking it would be locked and it opened. My eyes grew wide when I looked inside.

"Police. Stay where you are." I heard from downstairs. Who the fuck called the cops on me? I started panicking and jumped out the window. I ran to my car through the back and sped outta there.

****

"Did you get it?" Lina asked with a grin on her face when I came in the door.

"YOU SET ME THE FUCK UP BITCH!" She took off running. I started to chase after her.

CLICK! I froze and almost shit on myself when I saw who it was. These motherfuckers are about to kill me.

At the Restaurant

Remi

"What you mean did I know he killed your father?" I questioned Naima because I had no fucking idea what she was talking about.

"Years ago, my father was out with a few people he was cool with. Something happened that I still don't know about and my father was murdered. A man was arrested for his murder and his name was Remington Stevens." I turned to my father and his head was down. My mother had tears in her eyes along with my girl and her mother. What the hell is going on and why is it a damn crying fest out here?

"How could you do that me Remi?" I swung my head back to Naima.

"First off... I wouldn't do that to you. Second... I have my father's name. Why didn't you say something?"

"It didn't dawn on me because you always called him your pops. I never put two and two together."

"Come here." I grabbed her hand and walked away. We stopped a few cars down because with the way everyone was staring at each other I didn't want anyone fighting. I tilted her head back and made her look at me.

"Naima, I swear I didn't know my father took yours away. If I did, I would've told you."

"But you didn't." Now she was starting to aggravate me. I just told her I didn't know. My pops explained how the situation went down; however, I didn't know it was her father.

"Look, maybe your mom should explain what really happened because things aren't what they seem."

"You saying your father didn't do it?" She folded her arms across her chest.

"I'm saying you need to explore deeper into the night in question."

"Remi why is bad things happening to me? First your brother shows me a video of the bitch feeling all over you in the other club. Then, he tried to hug me and when I pushed him off, he chased up the steps behind me and squeezed my ass. I smacked him because that's a violation and he choked me." As

31

she told her story I became angrier. I saw him choking her and didn't know why.

"The woman approaches you, grabs your waist and calls you baby. It's like everyone is out to hurt me for loving you. Last but not least, I find out you're the son of the man who took away my father. Remi, I don't know what to do. I feel like I'm gonna lose it at any moment." I pulled her close and hugged her.

"You're gonna be fine." I moved her back, lifted her face and kissed her.

"How can I be in love with the son of a man who did that?"

"What happened in the past doesn't define what we got going on. Go home with your mom and let her tell you the truth. I'll be by after this is over and pick you up." She nodded and it made me feel better. I led her to the car and stopped when this bitch came over.

"Remi this is what you left me for?" I ignored her and so did Naima.

"I'm saying. You could've at least let me finish sucking you off earlier." My girl squeezed my hand tighter.

"What you say?" Naima asked and I saw this going bad.

"You heard me. We were having a moment at the other club. I was rubbing all over his chest, kissing his stomach like I always do and we almost fucked had he not smelled something burning." Monee had the nerve to smile.

"Is that right?"

"It's exactly right. That's why I'm confused why he sweating you when I'm here. Shit, I'll take him off your hands with no problem." Naima laughed.

"You do that then." She turned to me.

"Stay away from me Remi and I mean it." I pulled my gun from my waist, gripped Monee by the hair and had the gun on her side.

"I swear to God you better tell my girl right now with your lying, lactose intolerant for dick ass, or I'll shoot you in the side and watch you bleed out." Naima gasped and everyone came rushing over. I never wanted her to see me this way, but someone will always make you come outta character

"I did everything I said but he pushed me off. His dick never got hard. Oh my God Remi please don't kill me." She cried.

"Now its don't kill me. I told you not to fuck with my girl." I cocked the gun back. I was about to shoot her stupid ass.

"Son lets go. You got a bunch of people inside. This is not how you do business." I tossed Monee on the ground and looked at Naima.

"I'm not gonna sweat you." I put the gun in my waist.

"If this ain't what you want then it is what it is. I can't be out here doing this to prove you're the only one I want. I worked too hard for my shit." I started walking backwards.

"This is why I never claimed a bitch. They too much trouble and I lose focus."

"Whoa son. You know I don't play that disrespectful shit." My father and mother were in my face.

"I'm sorry you feel that way and don't worry, I won't ever bother you again." Naima yelled out and looked down at Monee before hock spitting on her.

Monee jumped up and unfortunately, caught the wrath of Naima. She walked the dogs with her. That's what Monee gets. I bet she won't say shit else to her.

"Feel free to have him." She barked after my father lifted her up. She went to her mom's car, sat down and I could see how hard she was crying. At this moment, I couldn't worry about anything but my restaurant.

"How did you get out Remington?" Her mom questioned on the way to her car.

"We'll talk but you need to tell your daughter the truth." She remained silent and pulled off. All of us walked inside and my brother was just getting off the ground.

"Where is Cat?" I asked. He still wasn't here, and I know he wouldn't miss it.

"His mom hasn't gotten back yet." My aunt said.

"You keep hitting me for a bitch who don't give a fuck about you." Ivan spoke with blood coming out his mouth.

"What nigga?"

"She was downstairs hugging me and got upset when I told her we weren't sneaking behind your back." I shook my head. Is he really tryna say Naima is like Nelly? He on some other shit for real.

"Nice try nigga. She already told me what happened." I moved closer.

"We may be going through something right now due to your childish behavior but make no mistake brother." I looked him up and down.

"If you even think about bothering her, I'm gonna keep my word and kill you. Fuck with me if you want." I pushed him so hard he fell off the stool he sat on.

"Oh, and don't expect another dime from me motherfucker so the bitch whose rent you been paying is no longer happening."

"WHAT?" My mom yelled.

"He didn't tell you?"

"Ugh no." She showed disappointment on her face.

"Yea he got some chick shacked up at an apartment and he's been paying her rent. Well I've been paying her rent because his ass broke." I was mad as hell when I found that shit out the other day.

After I made the decision to stop enabling him, I hired a private investigator to look into his finances and he came up with a ton of stuff; including having an apartment and another car. They're both in his name but he doesn't use either. I didn't understand why he stayed with my mom when he had a spot.

The investigator told me he stopped by the place and a woman answered the door. He asked who she was but wouldn't give her name and said the place is hers. I had every intention to go and kick her out tomorrow, which I'm still gonna do.

"I don't know what you talking about." I let a grin creep on my face.

"Then it won't be a problem kicking her out?" I walked back into the front where everyone was and put on my game face. I'm not about to let anyone ruin my night; even though they already did.

"Even after the fiasco earlier, you pulled it off." My cousin Tara sat next to me at the bar. It was after one in the morning and the staff just finished cleaning up. The event was only for a couple of hours.

"Drink?" I asked and poured her a patron shot. She loved them.

"I'm happy it's over." She nodded and swirled on the barstool.

"Naima called me."

"Oh yea?" I took a sip of my drink.

"Yea she said someone broke in her mother's house and broke down the walls."

"Say what?" I sat next to her.

"Yup. She said the person found a safe her or her mother knew nothing about."

"A safe? What was in it?" Why in the hell is someone breaking down walls in her house? I wonder if this has to do with the person blowing up her car and showing up in the hospital room.

"Evidently, Nothing."

"Nothing?" I questioned. If a person went through all that, they were definitely looking for something.

"Whoever went in her house, found it and removed the contents if there was anything in it." I lifted the cup to my lips.

"No one is gonna go through the trouble of breaking down walls if there wasn't anything in it."

"The same thing I said. But anyway, she wanted me to tell you she apologizes for messing up your night and to wish you the best of luck with all your future endeavors." She turned to me. I stood and walked to the window.

"Are you really done with her?" I rubbed my goatee and stared out at the river. The water was rough and splashing against the deck. It made me think if the waters can be rough one minute and calm the next, it means the storm is over. Could I look at my love life the same? Can Naima and I weather this storm brewing, or should I keep it moving?

"For now, yea. We need a break."

"Remi, I'm your cousin and I've been around you long enough to know you love her."

"Of course I do but it's too much shit going on."

"That's why y'all need to stay together." She came and stood by me.

"Remi don't let these hateful motherfuckers break y'all up."

"She broke up with me Tara." She agreed.

"She's scared."

"Scared of what? I never gave her any type of inclination I cheated or needed to cheat on her."

"Imagine falling in love with a man and seeing a video of another woman touching him." I gave her a look.

"Regardless if nothing happened it didn't look right. Then, the bitch shows up here and let's not forget Ivan stalking her. Its a lot to handle and last but not least, she just found out about uncle Remi. What do you expect?" I didn't say anything.

"Give her some time. She loves you and you feel the same. Y'all are meant to be together." She walked away and went behind the bar to make another drink. I sat down and thought about what she said. If its meant for us to link back up, we will. I picked my phone up and called Cat again. This time his mom answered.

"OH MY GOD REMI! I WAS JUST ABOUT TO CALL YOU." Her yelling in the phone made me stand.

"Something bad happened to Joseph and Ivy's missing. They broke in her house and blood is everywhere and..."

"Where are you?" My heart was beating fast as hell.

"The hospital. Remi this is bad. Please get here." I hung up, grabbed Tara, locked up and flew to the hospital. I hope Cat and Ivy's ok because if not, all hell is gonna break loose.

Cat

"IVY! IVY!" I shouted when our hands separated. I didn't give a fuck about anything but finding her. I knew she couldn't do much with her stomach still hurting.

POW! POW! More and more gunshots were ringing in the air. Who the fuck brought this to her house" I started shooting blind and prayed Ivy was hiding because the smoke from the bombs engulfed the house and I couldn't see a damn thing.

"Wendy said he wouldn't be here. Yo! Tha fuck." I heard a guy yelling.

"Wendy?" I whispered to myself as I slowly crept behind the dude. It was hard to see but since we were now outside, I had a better view. I had no clue who he was nor do I care at this point. All I wanted was my girl back and pray she wasn't hurt.

"Where the fuck is she?" I pressed the gun behind his head. He put his hands straight up.

"Who?" I hated for a nigga to play stupid.

"Don't who me nigga. The bitch who sent you. Where is she?"

"I don't know."

BAM! I hit his ass hard as hell across the face.

"A'ight man. She left with her cousin."

"Oh she was here?" I was shocked she didn't reveal herself and left people behind. The real question is how the fuck did Wendy pull this off?

"She stayed in the truck so her cousin could get your girl." My heart was racing at thos point. It made me wonder if he'd rape her, or even kill her.

"Where did they take her?" He didn't answer. I shot his ass in the side.

"Ahhhhh." He screamed out.

"Where did they take her?" I questioned again.

"She built a shallow grave for her somewhere. The plan is to bury her alive."

"FUCK!" I started pacing.

"Where is the place?"

"I don't know. It's outside of town somewhere. Can you get me some help?" I know his pink ass didn't just ask me for help.

"HELL NO!"

POW! I shot his ass in the head and fell to the floor when I tried to walk back in the front door. I needed to call Remi.

"POLICE FREEZE!" I put my hands up and watched different officers run inside.

"Shit. Joseph you ok?" One of the cops asked. I was happy someone knew me because if I die at least they'll know who to contact first.

"OH MY GOD!" I heard my mother shout behind me.

"WHERE'S IVY?" And there goes her mom. What were they doing here?

"Joseph are you ok? What happened?"

"Ma'am you can't be here." One of the officers said.

"I'm fine ma. I have to go." They all gave me a crazy look right before I passed out.

****

"You good bro?" I opened my eyes to see Remi standing over me, along with my mother, Ivy's mom and Tara. I surveyed the room and my girl was nowhere in sight.

"Shit. I have to go." I felt monitors all over and started ripping them out.

"Hold on yo. What you doing?" Remi tried to hold me there.

"I have to find Ivy."

"We've been looking for her? You know where she at?" Remi asked and they all waited for an answer. I knew this would make her mom lose it.

"Wendy set the shit up and took her." I told them in disbelief myself.

"Wendy? Took her?" Remi asked probably in shock like I was.

"Yea and they buried her in a shallow grave. Ain't no way in hell I'm staying here." I tried to get up again and Remi wouldn't let me.

"OH MY GOD!" Her mom screamed out.

"What's going on in here?" The doctor came running in because the monitors were beeping.

"I gotta go."

"Sir, you've been shot in the abdomen. It's not a good idea for you to leave." With my adrenaline pumping, I didn't realize my stomach was bandaged, nor did I know I was shot.

"Too got damn bad."

"Did he say where she was? What town or anything close to the spot?" Remi continued asking questions.

"No. Remi you gotta find her." I laid back on the bed when they slipped something in my IV. It must've been a sedative because my body started feeling weird.

"Yo! Meet me outside the hospital." I heard him on the phone talking to someone and felt myself getting upset. If anything happened to Ivy, I wouldn't forgive myself.

"Where is she?" Naima barged in the room. She stopped when her and Remi's eyes connected. Neither of them spoke, which is odd.

"I'll be back." Remi walked out the room and Naima moved over to my side of the bed.

"What's going on with you two?" Now it was my turn to ask questions.

"Let's worry about Ivy." I sat up a little and even with my eyes struggling to stay open, I wanted to know.

"I have no doubt my brother will find her. Tell me what's going on? Why aren't you speaking?"

"His father murdered mine." I heard the gasps in the room. Naima fell into the chair.

"Then his brother squeezed my ass, I smacked him, and he choked me. Oh, and the little ho from the bar that night we went out started some shit." No one said a word.

"I don't know how much longer I'll be able to speak with this medicine they put in me but one thing I know is, he ain't fucking no other bitch. As far as your father, even I know you need to speak with your mom. The Monee bitch is hateful. She ain't no threat. Trust me."

"To be honest, I know she's not. I was mad she put him in a situation to be caught up. My mother hasn't been able to tell me anything because someone broke in our house and it's just so much going on, I feel like we need a break."

"How does he feel?"

"Besides him saying he's not gonna sweat me and this is why he doesn't claim bitches, I'd say he's ok with it." She let her head fall against the window. I could see her wiping the tears.

"He's in love with you Naima and even though I wasn't there, I know it's not over."

"You didn't hear him Cat. He's done."

"Let me take you outside Naima. As we can see, Cat needs to rest." I heard Tara say before I could respond. I'm glad she did because I fell straight to sleep. Whatever they gave me was strong as hell.

Mario

"You set me up bitch." Is all I remember before being knocked over the head from behind. I opened my eyes and the room was pitch black. I couldn't see shit nor could I move. My body had to be tied to a chair because not only am I sitting, my hands are restrained.

"Yo! What the fuck!" I shouted to see if maybe someone stood outside the door or may have been watching me from a camera. Complete silence.

"YOOOOO!" I shouted again. Nothing.

Just as I went to open my mouth, the locks on the door clicked. The door opened and the sun beamed through. The only thing visible were two bodies that appeared to be men by their build.

"Finally woke up?" One headed in my direction while the other one walked in a different one.

"LIGHTS!" The guy shouted and I sucked my teeth. They had Lina in a holding room with a chain around her leg.

"Doesn't seem like you care what happens to her." He sat down across from me.

"Would you if she placed your loved ones in danger?"

"Point taken." He nodded and outta nowhere, I saw a bullet go into her forehead.

"To be honest, I can't say I'm hurt. It was her or my kids."

"Or Naima." He added and lit a cigar.

"It's no secret you love her but let me be the first to tell you, the nigga she with now ain't about to let you have her back." He shook his head.

"Nah. He's head over heels in love with her. I mean he threatened his brother's life over her and almost killed some bitch who thought she'd come in between."

"I don't wanna hear this shit." I may have done her dirty, but I don't wanna know nothing about her and another nigga.

"Whatever that woman has, had the man ready to murder for her. But then you know that from the gym." I gave him a fake smile. He really did find out everything.

50

"I thought Lina was your cousin." I changed the subject.

"She is but when you show disloyalties, then family means nothing." Who the fuck are these people and why didn't I meet them a long time ago?

"Huh?"

"The bitch called the cops on you because you hung up on her. How you think they knew you were there? Naima's mom lives in a single-family home and whether the sledgehammer was loud or not, no one would hear." He's right. She did live in a single-family home and the other house on both sides weren't far but far enough not to have heard.

"Are my kids ok?"

"That's up to you." He took another puff of his nasty smelling cigar.

"What do you want? I did like you asked and..."

"You did but the merchandise never came home with you."

"WHAT? I had the papers in my pocket. That's the only thing her father had in there."

It's partly true. The only other thing in the safe was a photo of five men standing in front of something. What? I have no idea. There was also a DVD. I figured it was Naima as a baby and her father didn't want it destroyed so I left it.

"Did you see money or a certain piece of jewelry?"

"Jewelry? No but there was a photo of five men and a DVD." He scratched his chin.

"If there was anything else it wasn't in the safe."

"I think he's telling the truth." The other guy said.

"Look, if you want, I can tell Naima it was me because I was saving my kids. She'll give me the DVD and picture. Whatever else you're looking for isn't there. Are you sure her father had it and not someone else?" He seemed to be thinking.

"You positive nothing else was there besides those three things."

"Positive. Listen if it were, I would've grabbed it. The only reason I didn't take the other two is because I figured the photo is of her father and the DVD had her baby stuff on it."

"If you're lying…"

"You can say and think whatever you want about me but one thing I won't do is play with my kids' lives."

"Hmm." He said and I tried to ease his doubt.

"I admit doing foul shit growing up but my kids mean everything to me. I'd never risk their lives even though her stupid ass did." I was still mad the bitch called the cops.

"For now, we're gonna let you live."

"Where are my kids?"

"The two with Lina are with your mom and the other two are with theirs." I let the breath I was holding in, out.

"Thank you for not hurting them."

"Call Naima in a few days and go visit her. Try and see if she knows anything."

"You just said the dude bugging over her."

"He is but you and her have history. She'll let you in." He stood to leave as the other guy unhooked my hands. They disappeared before I even left my seat.

****

"Daddy." My daughter ran over to me when I got to my mothers. I hugged her and my son extra tight. Those motherfuckers made me find my own way home. I didn't care as long as I was alive it's all that mattered.

"What happened to your head?" She rushed to get me an ice pack.

"Can we go see sissy today?" She was talking about my other daughter.

"Tomorrow. Daddy needs to rest. Ma can you keep an eye on them while I lay down?"

"Go head. I got them." I kissed both of them again, took the ice pack and laid down in her room. My pops was at work so I was good.

I can't even tell you how long I slept but I do know my mother was staring at me when my eyes opened.

"What did Lina do?" I excused myself to use the bathroom and returned to tell her what happened.

"You should've stayed with Naima."

"I had no choice ma. You know how much I loved her, but it was a decision I couldn't waste time thinking about."

"I understand." She stood.

"One thing I know is you better get your stuff out the house and sign it back over to her." She spoke in a firm tone.

"I am. I already have a house a few blocks over."

"From where?"

"Here. Now that Lina's gone, I'm gonna need help with the kids when I work. Its better to be closer to you."

"Boy, I ain't no babysitter." She shouted in Spanish and walked out the door. I wasn't worried about it because she loved all her grandkids and would do anything for them. With their mom gone, I know she'll help even more. I went downstairs and sat on the couch with the kids to watch television. I pray those people find what they're looking for.

Ivy

"Please don't do this." I shouted to Wendy who had her cousin tossing dirt on me. I had to keep my head down to avoid it going in my eyes. When I first realized it was her, I wanted to beat her ass but with the humongous guy she had there was no way.

On the ride over here all she talked about is how Cat killed her new boyfriend and beat her up for bothering me. Therefore; I had to hurt for what he did. He needed to feel the hurt he put her through. I couldn't believe she had the nerve to want someone to feel sorry for her after all the harassment and threats she had thrown towards me. The fights, coming to my job and all the other bullshit she did. People never want to take responsibility for their own shit and blame everyone but themselves.

"SHUT THE FUCK UP!" The guy barked and tossed more and more dirt. I moved as much as I could, but it didn't matter.

The amount of dirt began piling up and my waist was now stuck. I may have been able to move but not too much with my foot. I held my hands up so when he finished throwing the dirt on me, I could try something. What? I don't know but at least my hands would be free.

"PLEASE LET ME OUT!" I screamed and screamed until my voice was no longer there. The dirt went to my chest and sadly it started to rain. It wasn't storming but enough fell to turn the dirt into mud. All I could do is pray someone found me.

I felt the tears falling down my face as I began thinking about my mom, Cat and everyone else. If no one finds me I'll never have kids, I'll never walk down the aisle, I'll never do a lot of things and the only person to blame is Wendy and the guy she brought. It made me think about Cat and if he's alive. Is he's looking for me, does he think I'm dead or does he even care? What am I saying? Of course he cares. I may not appreciate how this is playing out with his ex, but I know he loves me.

After a good five minutes of feeling sorry for myself, I tried lifting my body over the dirt and felt stupid. My foot was in extreme pain and no matter how hard I tried to block the pain, nothing worked. I stood in the same position and cried my eyes out. I cried for my man, my mom and my life that was being taken away due to jealousy. She can say it's over Cat killing her man, but we all know the truth. She wanted him back and he wasn't beat.

"What the?" I basically whispered loudly because my voice was gone. I couldn't scream even if I wanted to.

Bugs were crawling over me and each time I flicked one away, another one came. I began imagining every bug in the world was crawling on me and started panicking. With every bit of strength I had, I pushed myself up by placing my hands on the dirt. It hadn't turned to mud yet; therefore, it was soft and \ I wasn't slipping and sliding.

"Lord if you help me outta this, I promise to say my prayers every night." I said to myself as I continued pushing up. My foot felt like it was going to fall off.

I finally made it to the top of the dirt, yet I was still in the ditch. I reached my hand over the top and dug my hands in the ground until I pulled myself out. I balled up in a fetal position and cried my eyes out.

The rain continued hitting me and still I didn't move. At this point my foot no longer had feeling in it and the only thing that matter is being out of the ditch. I looked up at the sky and thanked God because he's the only reason I made it.

The rain began to come down harder and I had no coat or anywhere to go. I glanced down at the ditch and couldn't believe how the dirt turned into a mud pool. If I had waited any longer, I'd probably be dead.

Searching the area with my eyes, I saw a piece of blue tarp. I drug my body over with my foot dangling, put it over me and laid there. It'll be daytime soon and hopefully someone rides down this way and sees me.

****

BEEP! BEEP! BEEP! BEEP! I heard and my eyes shot open. The sound of a truck backing up forced me awake.

"HOLD UP!" Someone shouted.

"IVY!" I thought my ears were deceiving me. I had to be hallucinating because no one knew where I was.

"IVY!" The person shouted again. I couldn't walk or speak. The only thing I could do is sit up and wave this tarp. The sky was still a tad bit dark and I couldn't see any faces.

"OH SHIT!" Footsteps could be heard running towards me.

"Cat is gonna bug the fuck out. You ok?" Remi said and tried lifting me. I punched his back over and over.

"What's wrong?" I pointed to my foot. Remi and the three other guys mouths dropped. It must be bad if their faces look like that.

"I'm gonna lift her and you two grab her legs. Don't let them fall." He looked at me.

"It's gonna hurt Ivy." I nodded, wrapped my arms around his neck and cringed at the pain with each movement.

"Take the truck back and meet me at the hospital." Remi told the guys who helped him place me in the back seat. I wanted to ask where Cat was and how he found me, but nothing came out.

"You're gonna be fine Ivy and Cat will be too." I wiped the tears falling from my eyes as he drove slow to the hospital.

When we arrived, Remi ran in and had the nurses and doctors come get me. Their facial expressions were the same after staring at my foot. Or it could be I'm covered in dirt and look like shit. Whatever the case, I didn't care. I'm happy I didn't die out there.

"OH MY GOD YOU FOUND HER!" My mom shouted running towards me. She held me tight and broke down. Naima, Tara and Cat's mom walked behind her and did the same. I noticed the tension between my best friend and her man. Neither of them spoke; yet, couldn't keep their eyes off each other. I looked at Naima.

"I'm glad you're ok. We'll be here when you come out." She knew I wanted to know what happened and ignored my look. She'll tell me later. I thanked Remi again, laid back in the bed and let them cart me away.

Naima

"I'm gonna go home and change. Let Ivy know I'll be back." I told her mom and hugged her.

"She's probably going to be asleep for a while. Come up tomorrow Naima."

"After everything you been through, you need to relax." She kissed my forehead.

"You coming ma?" Her and Margie came up not too long after I called. We were all pretty close and it hurts to see my best friend not only in pain but she almost lost her life.

"I'm going to stay. I'll see you at home." My mom said and Margie said she's leaving in an hour or so and she'd call me tomorrow.

I said my goodbyes to Tara and Cat's mom before leaving. I don't know why but my feet stopped in front of Remi. He was standing there pecking away at his phone. I noticed he had on a swear suit and hell yea I looked down. His print was visible, and a bitch hated it. He's working with a monster and I didn't want any of these messy nurses to stare more than they were.

"Thanks for finding Ivy." Its only fair to thank him; especially when Cat isn't well enough to.

"Yup."

"Ok." I expected him to say more.

"You can box my things up at your place and I'll ask Tara to pick it up." He lifted his head. I had a few outfits and pajamas at his spot.

"For what?"

"We're no longer together and I didn't think you wanted any memories of me there."

"Let's go." He gripped my arm gently and walked outside.

"Naima you were right about needing space but I'm not going anywhere. We both have things going on and need to tackle those issues first."

"But I..." He stopped me from speaking.

"You've been through a lotta shit with your ex and the insecurities are there." I nodded.

63

"Then the shit with my pops and yours."

"I'm sorry Remi. I didn't try and bring you in my drama. And..." I broke down crying and once he hugged me, I felt his love. He had me follow him to my car. It was a long walk because of how many people were here and off to the side. I unlocked the door and he had me sit in the back seat.

"Nah. You need to handle this right quick." He pointed to his erection. Why is he horny at the hospital?

"We're out in the open." He grabbed my hand, slid my pants and panties down and sat me on top.

"Oh Gawddd." I gripped the front headrest and moved in circles.

"Fuck me like you love me." I chuckled because he loved that song.

"Yea. Bounce on it. Just like that." He lifted my hips up and down.

"I love you Remi." He yanked my hair back and forced me to look at him.

"I love you too Naima and we'll get through it. Shit..."
He bit down on my neck. His fingers were rubbing my clit and the orgasm was brewing.

"What you waiting for?" He asked and thrusted under me. The car was shaking, windows fogged and once I felt the pressure. I squeezed his thighs and let go.

"Oh gawddd." I moaned out and he squeezed my ass letting out his own silent moan.

"Sorry ma. Ain't no room to lift you off." He must've released inside me.

"I needed that." I said in between breaths.

"Me too." He smacked me on the ass and slid me over. I reached inside the glove compartment for napkins.

"It's still you and me Naima." He threw his tongue down my throat. I stopped him and pulled my clothes up.

"It's not enough room for a second round." He and I both knew the quickie was to get it out the way. The second time around would take much longer.

"Where you going?" He asked and pulled his clothes up.

"Home. My mom is staying with me because we don't know who broke into the house."

"What happened with that?"

"I don't know. When she came to your restaurant for the grand opening, in just that short amount of time someone broke in, knocked the walls down and removed a safe I didn't even know was there." He sat there listening to me explain.

"Something had to be in there they wanted."

"That's what I thought but my mom said what they're looking for she hid a long time ago."

"Wait! Did your mom know the safe was there?"

"Yup. She never told me and said certain things I didn't need to know."

"Figured."

"Why you say that?" He had me move on his lap and I rested my head on his shoulder.

"Your mother is keeping the past of your father a secret for some reason. Go home and demand answers."

"I'm not sure I wanna know." He lifted my head.

"If you plan on being in my life it's best you find out now. I can't have you uncomfortable around my pops."

"Don't leave me Remi." He smiled.

"You buying my house in exchange for this good dick?" I tried to move but he held me there.

"I'm not going nowhere but you need to find out about the past."

"Ok."

"You have the key to my house. We may be giving each other space but my door is always open for you."

"I don't wanna leave." I gripped his neck tighter.

"Ivy's mom is right about you needing to rest. Come back up tomorrow and you know where my bed is." He kissed me and we stepped out the car.

"Text me when you make it home." He leaned in my window for another kiss.

"Be careful Remi."

"Always." He walked in front of my car and I pulled off sexually satisfied and happy. At least he's not leaving me for good and he's right. I need to demand answers from my mom, and I will soon as she gets home.

****

"I see you two made up." My mother sarcastically said when I walked in the kitchen. Last night I had every intention of talking to her but she stayed at the hospital. I didn't realize how exhausted I was because I showered and went straight to sleep. Here it is the next day and I feel energized.

"Why you say that?"

"Unless someone else gave you that hickey, I'd say you made up." I moved past her and grabbed the orange juice out the fridge. I sat at the table, poured my cup, brought the plate of food in front of me and asked her to sit.

"What happened to my father and don't leave anything out?"

"You sure you're ready for the answer?" I gave her the *duh* look. I'm grown as hell and she should've told me a long time ago.

"Years ago, I dated this guy Julio. He was sexy and had a little bit of money." I shook my head.

"At the time I didn't care because he had my heart. Two years of pure bliss was ripped away when I found out he not only cheated on me but produced a child in the process. I was devastated, hurt and didn't want anything to do with him. He tried to reconcile but it was too late. I wasn't helping to take care of a child that was made during our relationship. If the kid was before us, that's different." I poured syrup on my pancakes and continued listening.

"Five maybe six years went by and I hadn't seen or heard from him which was perfect for me. Evidently, he got locked up in a different state and being we weren't together it was no need for anyone to let me know.

"Makes sense." I said.

"I met your father a few months later and we hit it off. He wined and dined me for two months before I gave it up." I sucked my teeth. Don't nobody wanna hear that.

"Anyway, we didn't use protection and I got pregnant right away." I dropped my fork.

"What?"

"Ugh Remi and I had unprotected sex last night and I forgot to grab the pill."

"Lucky for you, you have 24 hours. Hurry up and eat so you can get one." I nodded. Neither of us are ready for a child.

"Let me finish before you go." She blew her breath.

"I met Remington after your father and I slept together for the first time. He introduced him as his best friend and from that day on, the four of us were always around each other."

"The four of you?" I questioned.

"Me, your father, Remington and his girlfriend. We became best friends and I was in their small wedding."

"WHAT?"

"Yup. We go way back." I couldn't believe our parents were affiliated with one another. No wonder they gave each other those looks at the grand opening. They probably hadn't seen each other in years.

"Long story short, one night Remington and your father went out to a bar with two or three other people they knew, and Julio showed up. Somehow, he knew about your father and I and started talking shit. Now Remington and your dad we're heavy into the Muslim religion. Fighting is never their first option during a confrontation."

"Ok."

"They go outside, and Julio attacks your father which makes Remington jump in. The other guys get in and so does Julio's people. Your father beat Julio real bad. Unfortunately, the people with him didn't appreciate it and outta nowhere stabbed your dad over and over." I covered my mouth. My mom never explained in detail what went down. It's hard to hear.

"Remington went crazy and banged the guys head into the ground until he damn near busted it open. Some guy jumped on Remington and his wife snatched the knife from the other guys hand and killed him. The last guy was killed by Remington because he started choking his wife."

"Wait a minute." I stood and began pacing the kitchen.

"You're telling me, my father and Julio were fighting over you. Julio's friend got mad my father beat him up and stabbed him to death. Remington killed him and another man

71

for choking his wife and she killed someone for trying to kill him?"

"I'm afraid so."

"Why did his father go to jail for all those years?"

"One... Remington would never turn his wife in, and she couldn't testify for or against him. Second... there is a no snitching rule and he'd never allow his wife to open her mouth. And lastly... Julio disappeared; therefore, no other witnesses came forward. Well people did but they pointed the finger at Remington, which is why he was charged with your father's murder."

"Why didn't you tell me? I'm thinking Remi's father did this and took it out on him."

"Shit. I didn't know you'd meet the son."

"Oh my God. I have to apologize for the mix up." I ran in my room and rushed to get dressed. When I finished she handed me my purse and keys.

"Your phone is inside. Have fun and make sure you throw it on him. I need this condo to myself once you move in."

"MA!"

"What? I'm not going back to the house. This spot is convenient for me to get to work anyway. Now go ride that pony." I busted out laughing and ran to my car. I went to his house and his truck was gone so I drove to the Club Turquoise restaurant. I wanted to surprise him and that's where Tara said he was when I called her. The two of us were becoming very cool and I appreciated talking to her sometimes. She gave me more insight on the type of man Remi was. Hell, he wasn't gonna tell me.

I parked next to his truck and went in. Shockingly the door was open. I traveled downstairs and he wasn't anywhere in sight. I walked up the stairs and heard a woman's voice. I stopped at the door.

"Mr. Stevens, the small fire was considered arson and had you not been here it would've done more damage."

"How did it start?"

"It appears to be a match lit in the sink. The dish towel was set on fire and it went from there." It was complete silence for a few seconds.

"Thanks, and I'll let you know when the kitchen is fixed so you can come back to check it out."

"Remington when are you gonna stop playing and give me what I want?" I peeked in and this woman was literally unbuttoning her blouse.

"Yea Remi, when?" I stepped in for him to see me and shook my head in disappointment. I can't even be mad because I'm the one who said we needed space.

"FUCK!" He shouted.

Remi

"FUCK YO! PUT YOUR DAMN CLOTHES ON." I shouted at Victoria. She's the fire inspector and dropped by to bring me the report about the small kitchen fire.

I knew she was attracted to me for years but never took the bait. She's ok looking but any woman who'd use her job to catch niggas ain't my type. I mean if she doing it with me there's no telling how many other men she's done it with.

"Remi stop fighting it." She stood in front of me and grabbed my dick.

"Bitch, I said move." I pushed her out the way and ran down the steps to catch Naima. I had no idea she'd stop by and I wasn't mad either. I don't fuck in my office and this bitch caught me completely off guard.

"NAIMA!" She was getting in the car. I caught the door before she closed it.

"I don't wanna know and I'm not mad." I pulled her out the car and stood in front of her.

"Yes you are and you have every right to be." She turned her head and I turned it back.

"Space doesn't mean be with someone else. Victoria…"

"Victoria?" She questioned with sarcasm.

"Yes Victoria. She's had a crush on me for years. She wants to know why I won't give her dick." She rolled her eyes.

"I don't want her or anyone else but you." That captured her attention.

"Can't nobody get this unless you give it away." She finally put her arms around my neck.

"I want you too and I came by because my mother told me everything."

"She did?" I kissed her neck.

"Yea." Her hands we're going to up the back of my shirt." My dick was starting to grow.

"I never fuck in my office but since you're here and he's awake, I'll make an exception." Her hands moved to the front of my jeans

"Yea he's awake.

"So you fucking the help anyway and won't give me none." My dick shriveled right up listening to her.

"Excuse me." Naima said.

"I know who you are Ms. Health Inspector. I wonder what they'll say when they find out you're screwing people to get your businesses open."

"Bitch bye." She laughed.

"I'm serious. I mean why else would you be messing with a low budget woman?" She gave Naima a nasty look after staring her up and down.

"Low budget says the woman who wants to fuck my man. The same man who told you no years ago. The same man who knows if you'll throw yourself at him, you'll do it with others." I had to snap my neck because I literally just told her that.

"You can go tell anyone you want about our relationship but just know I'm about to ride the shit outta this dick you were tryna hop on."

"Mr. Stevens you allow your so-called woman to speak this way?"

77

"Like she said Victoria. She's about to ride this ride, so bounce." I grabbed Naima's hand, walked inside, locked the doors and fucked the shit outta her in my office.

"No more pussy for you until we're back together." She said coming out the bathroom.

"We are together. You're just at your place and I'm at mine." I told her staring at the email on my computer.

"Well, we're not together until you apologize for calling me a bitch and we sleeping in the same bed." I looked over and she sat on the couch naked with her legs wide open.

"You play all day Naima."

"I'm just saying. You said bitches make you lose focus and..." I removed my clothes again and stood in front of her stroking myself.

"You do make me lose focus and I apologize for calling you a bitch. Damnnnn." Her mouth was wrapped around my dick and she deep throated the hell outta me. Oh yea we back together.

****

"You do know they're not going to stop coming for her until Nyeemah's dead or returns whatever they were looking for?" My pops said with my mom sitting on his lap. Ever since he came home, they've been inseparable in and out the bedroom.

"Why do they want her mom dead and what they looking for?"

"Julio blames Nyeemah for his brother dying and vowed to avenge his death."

"She wasn't even there."

"Exactly." My mom chimed in.

"He wants a reason to be around her and he's looking for money and some piece of jewelry he claims Naima's father had."

"Jewelry and he died years ago." I questioned because he was going real hard for someone looking for jewelry."

"Supposedly, Julio's brother gambled a lot and, in the process, lost their fathers ring. He wants it back and Nyeemah has it." My father told me and I looked at him.

"Why does she have it?"

"Because he lost it to Naima's father. He wouldn't return it because it was a fair loss." My father shrugged his shoulders.

"All this for a ring tho?"

"The ring is worth a lotta money. I'm talking about in the millions."

"Really?" My mom asked.

"Yea. The stone is from Africa or someplace like that and it's huge. Like I said, Julio's brother lost it over a fifty-dollar bet."

"Damn." I shook my head.

"No one knew it was worth that kinda money and we still wouldn't if Julio didn't find his fathers will a few years ago. It described the origin of the ring and when Julio questioned people about it, it was indeed true."

"How'd you find out and why didn't he take it?" My father smirked.

"I may have been in jail but it's nothing I didn't know about. As far as anyone taking it, Naima's cousins and a few uncles are in the streets; therefore, someone has always been watching them. And being my best friend, I had people keeping an eye on them too."

"Why didn't you mention her?"

"Boy you were always outta town or country. You are the last person I expected to end up with her." I laughed.

"What's so funny?" Ivan stepped in the kitchen in just basketball shorts.

"None of your got damn business." I barked.

"Oh you still mad your girl tried to fuck me at your job?" I hopped out my seat.

"I told her no, so relax. It won't be the same as with Nelly."

"Tha fuck you want from me Ivan? Huh? I gave you everything you wanted because pops wasn't able to. You got a car, money, jobs etc. and you still not happy. Does *my perfect life* as you say bother you?"

"Remi calm down." My mom got in between us.

"Ma, he needs to speak his peace and move the fuck on. I'm tired of this jealousy shit."

"Jealous?" How this nigga act as if he were offended?

"Nigga please. Jealous of what? I got your girl all those years ago and I can get your new one if I want." I balled my fist up.

"Oh you mad? So what you gave me those jobs, you still ain't shit but a washed up dope dealer who used his money to open up businesses. Businesses I helped stay open. I was there when you weren't. It was me, not you." I had to chuckle at hos ignorance because he had no fucking clue.

"Ok. How much money did you put down since we discussing what you did? How many people did you deal with during the construction, inspections, banks and furnishing the place, along with the staff? Let me know because I missed that." I folded my arms in front of him.

"I didn't need you to run shit nigga because I had managers and if they couldn't do it, I could. I gave your dumb ass the opportunity to run a business in hopes of opening your own and let you do it yourself but no. You fucked up anything I put you in charge of because you couldn't control your mouth.

"Remington stop them." My mom told my father.

"No. This has to happen. Get from in between them."
He moved my mom which gave me space an opportunity to beat my brother's ass.

"How long did you sit on those corners with me to make the money you claim is from this dope dealer? Huh? Tell me motherfucker." He stood quiet. My anger was building by the second.

"When ma couldn't afford to pay the rent and you graduated high school and worked at some store in the mall, how much money did you give her to help?" He didn't wanna go to college and literally worked at the mall for a month and a half. Talking about they don't pay enough. From that day on he only accepted money from me and worked in places I put him at.

"Nothing nigga. You said your check was yours and she needed to find a man because her husband was in jail taking dick up the ass."

"WHAT!" My pops was pissed. I never mentioned it and obviously my mom didn't either.

"I'm the one who stepped up." He tried to wave me off and I smacked his hand down.

"Yea, the twelve-year-old whose brother fucked his girlfriend because he couldn't get his own bitch." I looked him up and down.

"Yea I know all about your little dick having ass." My mom gasped.

"Bitches talk and since you popping shit, ask the Nelly bitch why every time she sees me she tryna fuck and suck me off." This nigga had me hot.

"The bitch you bragging about will fuck whatever nigga got the most money."

"Fuck you punk. She don't wanna fuck you."

"Yea a'ight. I bet if I pulled my dick out in front of her she'd dropped to her knees." Now it was his turn to get mad.

"If she did then why she stay with me all these years?" I had to laugh at his stupid ass again. He's asking questions he should have the answer to.

"Because of the money this dope dealer gave you." I pointed to myself.

"The money I gave you had her believing yo ass was rich."

"No it's not." He said tryna make himself believe it.

"Oh, it is brother. She damn sure ain't around for that little ass dick you sticking in her and everyone else." He moved in the other room and I followed. This conversation needed to be had and we can move on.

"This is why I can't work for you. All you do is throw your money in my face. You did this, you did that."

"NIGGA, I WOULDN'T IF YOU DIDN'T BRING UP THE FAKE SHIT YOU DID."

"Whatever."

"Now it's whatever. Ma, I'm out because he about to make me knock his ass out again." I headed to the door.

"Watch that new bitch. She loved when I squeezed her ass and I'm sure she'll be down if I whisper sweet nothings in her ear." He shouted and I took off after him. My father had to grab me.

"Go home son. He's tryna get a rise outta you. We all know Naima ain't thinking about his ass."

"One more time pops and I swear he's mine." He pushed me out the door.

"Call your woman and let her calm you down." I busted out laughing.

"What nigga? I told you when that woman finds you, she gonna have you stuck and Naima is her."

"How you figure?"

"You were about to murder him over saying that shit. And you beat his ass twice over her already. I know what it is."

"Bye pops." I got in my car and called Naima. I'm about to let her calm me down alright. Calm me down as I'm in that pussy but I need to make a quick stop.

Ivan

"Ivan, I don't know what's come over you." My mother said as my father pushed Remi out the door.

"Your perfect fucking son is my got damn problem. He can do no wrong to you, can he?" I stared at my mother giving me a *are you crazy speaking to me this way* look. I try not to ever disrespect her but when it comes to Remi, she always defends him, and I find myself talking shit to her. It's not right but I can't help it.

"Ivan your brother isn't around to show me if he does bad things. Even as a kid he hid a lot of things from me."

"Not the money."

"You a'ight in here?" My father asked giving me the look of death.

"We ok babe. We're just talking." He kissed her cheek and walked out. I was happy because I don't need him in here tryna control the conversation. I loved my pops but I feel like he left it on us to take care of the household because he was in the streets being reckless.

"How could he hide the money when he was the one helping with the bills? He's the one who risked everything to make sure we had because your father couldn't."

"You're telling me it was ok for him to bring the drug money in the house?"

"Ivan, I wasn't ok with how he made his money and its unfortunate to see my child resulted in the drug world in order to help his family. I tried countless times to make him stop and what did he do?" She folded her arms across her chest.

"Exactly. I grounded him a hundred times, threw away the dope when I found it hidden in his room, even beat his ass once so don't you dare stand here and insinuate, I was ok with it."

"You accepted the money." She scoffed up a laugh.

"When I realized my son was going to do what he wanted, I sure did and guess what?" She moved closer to me.

"What?"

"Your ass did too. I didn't see you having a problem putting your hand out. You wanted the new sneakers, a new car, wardrobe and whatever else you asked for he brought because

88

you were his brother. Hell, he even gave you money for the women you misrepresented yourself to as this rich guy." I waved her off.

"And let's be clear on how the money was giving to me. Remi snuck and went to the pawn shop with the bills and paid them. He went to the office in the projects and paid the rent. So don't make it seem like he handed me money in the beginning." I was over this conversation at this point because she's not seeing it from my point of view. No one ever does.

"What do you want son? Are you missing something? Why are you against anything Remi does?"

"FUCK REMI! HE AIN'T SHIT BUT A NIGGA YOU BIRTHED." I don't know why that triggered me.

WHAP! She smacked me so hard, my face turned.

"Did you just smack me?" I walked up on her.

"You walking up on me like you wanna fight." She pushed me back and started taking her earrings off.

"Let's go son. I may be a woman, but I'll beat your motherfucking ass in here." She got in a fighting stance. I ran up on her and the punch to my face made me stumble back. I couldn't believe my mother punched me and the shit hurt too.

"Bring it on nigga." She said with disappointment.

"Oh hell no." I ran up on her again and almost died when I felt the hit to my ribs.

"I don't care if you're my son. I better not ever see you run up on my wife again." My father had his big arm around my throat.

"Do I make myself clear?" I used both hands to try and remove it, but nothing worked.

"Let him go Remington." My mom said and sat back down. I felt my body hit the ground and looked up to see her putting back on the earrings.

"Never in my life, did I think one of my own kids would run up and try to hit me."

"You hit me. I'm supposed to take that."

"You don't have to take shit. You got shit twisted if you think I'm gonna let my own child disrespect me? The child I laid up in the hospital giving birth to? Nah, you got me fucked up Ivan Stevens."

"I got you fucked up when you swung on me first."

"Answer me this son. If I were out on the street and a man approached me in a disrespectful way, would you even defend me?"

"Not if you were wrong like you are now. You had no fucking business hitting me." My father charged at me and she jumped in between us.

"You have to go Ivan."

"Go where ma?"

"You should've thought of that before tryna come for me."

"Oh, I see. Your husband home and you want the house to yourself so you can do all that fucking."

"I don't need you to leave for me to fuck my husband or do anything else for that matter. I want you to leave because you've become disrespectful towards me and the hatred you have for your brother is taking over your mind. You've become obsessed over his success and yet, done nothing to show and prove you can do the same." I sucked my teeth because here she is singing his praise again.

"Ivan, you have just as much brilliance in you as anyone else. Take the time to find yourself and start building up for the success I know you can have." I waved her off and limped towards the steps. She put her hands on me, praised Remi and then tells me I'm brilliant. She's a got damn hypocrite.

"I'll gladly leave because don't nobody wanna hear y'all fucking."

"Out of everything I just said to you, that's all you're worried about?" She questioned and I ignored her.

"Wrinkled up dick nigga." I put my foot on the first step and turned around.

"Mother you better check for AIDS. He's been in jail a long time." I put my finger under my chin.

"Maybe that's why he wouldn't allow you up there. His boyfriend wasn't tryna hear it."

"Oh you funny nigga." My pops said.

"Pretty much." I gave him a phony grin.

"REMINGTON NOOO!" I hauled ass upstairs when I saw him running towards me. He started banging on the door.

92

"Remington lets go in the room. He's leaving." I could hear her begging and thank God she was. He'd probably kill me if he gets his hands on me.

"That ain't my motherfucking son. I don't know where he came from!"

BOOM! He slammed the door and I felt the walls shake. Damn, is he Hercules.

I pulled out a couple duffle bags, the two suitcases in my room and packed my things in it and peeled out the door. I'm not scared of my father, but I can't beat him either. I put the straps of the duffle bags around my neck, lifted the two suitcases and left the house. I looked in the rear-view mirror and said goodbye to the place I called home for years. *Good riddance.*

****

"What you doing here?" Nelly asked and kept looking up the steps. Why she asking me questions anyway when I'm funding her lifestyle?

"I'm moving in."

"Ugh, no you're not." I sat my shit on the floor and walked in the kitchen. I grabbed a beer and took a seat on the couch.

"This apartment is in my name. I purchased everything in this bitch so yea, I'm staying." She rolled her eyes.

"Don't you mean I purchased everything in here?" I turned to see Remi coming down the steps zipping up his jeans. Did she fuck him? He went in the kitchen, washed his hands and stepped in the living room smiling.

"Bitch, I know you didn't sleep with him." I whispered so he couldn't hear me. She never got the chance to answer.

"The way I see it is, both of you are living off my money and if you plan on keeping it that way, I suggest you get ready to start paying rent." He glanced around the condo.

"Wait! Why all your stuff here?" He pointed to my things.

"I decided to give our parents their own space." I wasn't about to tell him what took place. He'd really kill me.

"Good. Your grown ass need to be on your own." I sucked my teeth.

"Why you wearing sunglasses in the house?" He questioned.

"Because I can. Why you here?" I barked softly so he wouldn't think I was getting smart. I don't need him tryna fight in front of her.

"I came by to see who the bitch was I'm taking care of. Who would've guessed it's the same bitch who you fucked all those years ago? Pussy must be good huh?" I ignored him.

"I hope she gets wet now and learned how to suck dick because whether I was a virgin or not, she couldn't fuck then either." He shrugged his shoulder and I could tell Nelly was embarrassed.

"Now Nelly, like I said before. No, we can not ever fuck, you can never suck my dick and I'll be damned if you'd be my side chick." Remi smiled as he said it. I looked at Nelly and her mouth was on the floor.

"Told you brother. She'll swing that pussy to any nigga with money. Y'all have a good night." He went to the door and turned.

"Don't think I forgot the bullshit you said at our parents' house. Trust, you will see me. And Nelly…" He gave her the once over.

"You picked the wrong brother to fuck with." He slammed the door behind him.

"Hey baby." She nervously said.

"Baby? Were you tryna fuck my brother?" I sipped my beer.

"No. He said it to get you mad." I didn't know if I should believe her or not.

"What's this about you spending his money and this is his place?" she took a seat next to me and started rubbing my chest. Its most likely to take the heat off her.

"I ain't about to talk about the lies he spitting out." Remi loved showing off.

"If they lies, why you nervous?"

"Bitch, shut the fuck up with all the questions." I rested my head against the seat tryna come up with ways to destroy Remi and not incriminate myself.

Ivy

"Hey beautiful." I opened my eyes and Cat was sitting in a wheelchair next to me. I could tell he's been crying due to the redness in his eyes.

"Oh my God! You're ok." He took my hand in his and wouldn't let go.

"Ahhhh!" I screamed out after moving my foot trying to sit up.

"Relax Ivy." I nodded and he wiped the tears falling down my face.

"I was so scared baby. I thought you were dead, and I was gonna die." He smiled and placed his hand on top of mine.

"It's in the past and I have to focus on you getting better to walk down the aisle."

"We're still getting married?" I heard footsteps coming towards us and turned my head. My mom, Remi, Cat's mom and Naima were here. I was so focused on seeing him I never paid it any mind.

"Thanks bro." Remi handed him something.

"You ready to take my last name?" He opened the small box that held a huge pink diamond and placed it on my finger.

"I don't know why you took so long asking me?" I joked and he gave me a dirty look.

"I'm just saying Cat. You could've asked me a few more times after the first one." Everybody started laughing and congratulated us.

"Can we have a minute?" Cat asked and they all stepped out. He stood from the wheelchair and scooter me over so he could sit next to me. It hurt like a bitch to move but I wanted him close. He let his lips crash on mine and we went at it like we could do something.

"You have no idea how happy I am to see you." He put his head on my forehead after saying it.

"What's wrong?"

"I need you to stay at my house or with your mom."

"What's wrong with my house?" I was concerned because everything I owned is there.

"Nothing baby but I can't risk anything happening to you again."

"What's really going on?"

"It's about to be a war out here and I need to know you're safe." I gave him a look to tell me more.

"I'm gonna kill Wendy, the guy who took you and anyone else involved." He said in a stern voice and I tensed up. I didn't wanna go through the idea of losing him again.

"Cat."

"Then some shit happened with Naima and Remi is on his own warpath looking for the people."

"Hold on. What did I miss?"

"We missed a lot at the grand opening, but I'll let Naima tell you the rest."

"I'm really lost because when Remi brought me here, they weren't even speaking." He pecked my lips.

"I'm gonna tell you like I told her. Remi is in love with Naima and he's not letting her go unless she did some unforgivable shit, which we know won't happen because she's not like that."

"Just please be safe with whatever you have going on. I won't be able to take it if you anything happens to you." I told him.

"I'm gonna always come home to you." We started kissing until we heard the doctor come in. He asked how I was doing and did a short examination.

Once he left, everyone walked back in and stayed until visiting hours were over. I cried when Cat had to leave because I didn't want to be without him. He called when he got home and we stayed on the phone for the rest of the night. Lord please keep him safe.

*********************.

"I can't believe the bitch sent people here." I said to Naima who brought me home to grab some things. Cat had some guy follow me because he was doing something with Remi and refused to allow us here alone.

I've been out the hospital for two days where he came home a day before me. I had to stay with my mother and trust me it was torture. I love her to death, but she does too much.

For instance, after Cat brought me there, she had wedding magazines in the bedroom for me, along with baby ones. When I asked why, she says, oh you can start looking. Plus, she needs to know what dress she's going to wear. Again, I love her to death but sometimes it's too much.

I asked Naima if I could stay at her place, but she said her mom is there. I didn't have an issue with it until she mentioned Nyeemah had a new man. Ain't no way I'm listening to her fuck. Say what you want but old people be getting it in these days; including my mother and her man.

"You know Cat is gonna get them." I pushed the crutches forward to walk and went into my home office.

"What you need?" Naima had a duffle bag on her shoulder. Everything I pointed to, she placed inside. Once it was full, she took it outside and returned to finish helping.

"Sooooooo, tell me what happened at the grand opening." I pried sliding on my ass up the steps. She began explaining and it was a mess. I couldn't believe the shit Remi's brother and the chick were going through for attention. It made me ask if they're working together because it damn sure sounds like it.

"And girl, Remi came to the house and fucked the shit outta me. It was good and rough but I could tell something bothered him." I sat on the bed pulling things out my nightstand.

"Well?" I questioned waiting for her response.

"Well Ivan has been allowing some chick to stay in a place Remi's footing the bill for."

"WHAT?"

"Bitch, that ain't the best part. Get ready for it." I ceased all movement and gave her my full attention.

"It's the bitch Nelly, Remi claimed as his first girlfriend."

"You fucking lying."

"Nope and when Remi stopped by to see who it was and mention them paying rent, the bitch tried to fuck and suck him off." She was mad as hell telling me the story.

"Oh hell no." I was annoyed listening to more shit Ivan was doing. He's like a fly that won't go away.

"I asked him for the address so I can beat her ass for hurting him all those years ago and trying to get him in bed. Of course he wouldn't tell me."

"You think he was hurt over it?" She sat next to me.

"He may not admit it and I doubt he loved her, but I think he was, only because it was his brother. Like Ivan, you know Remi had her there all the time and regardless of what she told him or what he thought, she should've been hands off."

"Hell yea. I wish my sister would."

"Bitch you ain't got one." Naima said laughing.

"Not the point." We both started laughing.

"Yea it's crazy because he definitely showed me the video of the bitch Monee feeling on Remi thinking it would make me want him. No thanks. I'd rather be single."

"I don't blame you Naima. It seems like Ivan is jealous."

"He really is. They got into it at his parents' house and that's before he found out about Nelly. I asked how did he calm himself and his crazy ass said because I knew you were gonna give me some bomb ass head." I laughed so hard my foot slid off the bed and hit the floor. Painful wasn't the word.

"Stop hurting yourself because I do not want to hear your man's mouth."

"Stop saying funny shit." She waved me off.

"Are y'all back together?" I asked because the way she's talking it seems like they are.

"I guess. He told me I better be in his bed every night or else."

"Or else what?"

"Who knows? He'll probably have me walking funny." She shrugged her shoulders and finished helping me pack.

By the time we left it was after five and I hadn't even started dinner. However, when I opened the door, Cat's mom and mine were in the kitchen drinking and cooking. As much as I wanted to complain, I couldn't. I appreciated the hell out of them for helping out.

"Hey sunshine." My mom called to me as I closed the door.

"Hey. Can you bring my food upstairs? My foot hurts and I wanna lay down."

"Sure honey. Go ahead we got this." His mom pointed up the steps.

"Thanks." I hopped on one leg going up because my ass still hurts from sliding at my house.

I opened the bedroom door and smiled. There were some flowers and heart candy on the bed. I swear all the rough times we had in the past he still knows how to make smile.

I took a hot bath with my foot hanging on the side and hopped in bed. My dinner was on a tray looking delicious. After I ate, I popped a pain pill and was knocked out.

Cat

"It feels good lying next to you." I told Ivy this morning. I came in late last night and didn't wanna bother her. I know her foot is in a lotta pain, which is more reason why I wanna find that bitch. I don't care nor do I wanna know how Wendy devised her plan. All I know is I'm gonna make her wish she were never born.

"It feels good lying next to you too; especially, after the things we've been through." She lifted her head to kiss me.

"I'm gonna be out the house most of the day and night. Remi said you can stay at his place with Naima when she gets off work or you can go to one of our moms' house. Either way you're not staying here alone."

"Did you find her?" I questioned about Wendy. I wanted him to kill her ASAP. I don't like this paranoia shit we have going on.

"I'm going to Ivy and I'm sorry she got you."

"You can't control it. I should've gotten the alarm system a long time ago like you told me. After all the bullshit, who knew she was capable of pulling this off?"

"Never underestimate what someone will do when they want something." She nodded and laid quiet.

"What you doing?" Ivy asked when I slowly climbed on top of her. Yea my stomach is still messed up, but I need some pussy.

"I'm about to make love to my girl and hopefully get her pregnant." She started laughing.

"I can't ride you."

"We can do it missionary all night for all I care. I just wanna be inside you." Thankfully she only had on a t-shirt.

"And I want you there." She smiled and made herself comfortable. Freaky sex may not be an option right now but who cares.

****

"You ready?" Remi asked looking at me. After sexing Ivy down, we went back to sleep and a nigga still tired.

"Yup."

107

"Next time no fucking first." He joked.

"What makes you think that?"

"You tired as hell and you ain't take no pain pills so what else could it be?" I waved him off and prepared myself to get the first nigga I saw. I glanced down at my stomach and felt the extra bandage to make sure no blood seeped through.

We stepped out the car, walked up to the door and he kicked it in. You heard someone yelling upstairs and an old lady was on the couch. Her eyes grew wide and terror was all over her face.

"Too bad you caught up in their shit." I said and shook my head.

PHEW! PHEW! I sent two to her head and we made our way up the steps.

"This nigga fucking." You could hear moaning over the radio. Remi opened the door and what do you know. The big motherfucker who took my girl was standing there hitting some chick from the back.

It took me a minute to find out who he was because I had no idea who Wendy had working with her. But after going through the hood asking questions, people started singing like canaries when money was offered. You can't trust a soul.

Anyway, it's the same cousin I couldn't stand years ago and tried to pop shit when I killed the dudes who robbed my house. One of those guys were related to them as well and lost their life. I don't understand why they mad at me when his own cousin got all of them caught in my wrath.

CLICK! I placed my gun on the back of his head.

"WHAT THE...?" He didn't finish his sentence because I split his eye with the butt of the gun.

"How you fucking her? She dry as hell." Remi snatched the girl off the bed by the hair. Not that we were looking but her pussy was wide open, and it did look dry as hell.

"Get dressed." I barked.

"I ain't going nowhere." He poked his chest out.

"Ok."

PHEW! Remi shot the girl in the head and this nigga lost it. I guess it was his girl because he started crying.

"See how it feels when someone comes in and takes the life of someone you love?" He snapped his neck to look at me.

"Fortunately, for you, my girl made it out alive, but I guarantee you won't." You could see fear on his face.

"Don't get nervous now. After all, you came in my girls' house, punched her in the face and attempted to bury her alive. It wouldn't be right if I didn't offer you the same courtesy." I hooked off and knocked his big ass out. Remi called the guys in who were waiting outside, and they drug him to the black van we had.

We drove to the exact spot Remi found her in which wasn't that far from town; yet, if you weren't looking for the spot, you definitely wouldn't have found it. I asked Remi how he did, and he said, they searched every vacant lot, deserted area, houses and anywhere else they could. He even had a big ass bulldozer truck in case they needed to use it to remove something off her. I appreciated the fuck outta him for finding her when I couldn't.

"Get up." I smacked dude in the face and waited for him to step out.

"I can tell you where Wendy is. Please don't do this." He cried and begged.

110

"Did you have compassion when my girl was most likely asking the same thing?" he put his head down.

"Exactly and like I said its only fair to bestow the same courtesy to you." I pushed him down in the ditch, in just his underwear. He didn't wanna get dressed at the house and nobody had time to dress his big ass. The boxers would do.

"Don't worry. Wendy will be joining you soon." I smiled. I had every intention of doing the same thing to her.

PHEW! PHEW! I shot him twice in the leg to make sure he couldn't climb out.

"Have fun in hell." The guys tossed the dirt on him and I asked them to fill it up halfway because Wendy needed a spot.

After we finished there, Remi and I drove to Wendy's spot. You could see her moving around in the house because like always she had the shades open. The bitch loved showing off her body. I never seen a woman seek as much attention as she does.

"What you wanna do?" Remi asked passing me the blunt.

"I'm tryna wait for Ivy to get better so she can do it."

"You know it's gonna be a while."

"I know. I'll leave her for now and see what Ivy wanna do. She may have me bring her to the ditch and wanna be the one who throws the dirt."

"A'ight." He pulled off and dropped me off at home.

"Hey babe." Ivy had a smile on her face as she rested on the couch.

"Hey. You need anything?"

"I should be asking you."

"Cat, you've been doing everything for me." She hugged me when I sat down next to her.

"Its nothing waiting on you Ivy. You're my fiancé and its what I'm supposed to do." We started kissing.

"You don't have to worry about Wendy's cousin anymore." I told her after moving back and resting my head on the couch. I still needed to take it easy after being shot but I hated to see my girl paranoid.

"And Wendy?" She questioned.

"I was gonna get her, but I wanted to know what you wanna do? I can kill her or let you do it."

"I dint even have the energy for it. Next time you see her, handle it and I'll make sure you reap great benefits." She unbuckled my jeans and had me moaning like a bitch. Oh how I appreciated the shit outta my woman.

Wendy

"What do you mean grandma and Brian are dead?" I shouted to my mom over the phone and froze at the same time.

"Someone went in grandma's house and killed her. I'm assuming Brian is dead too because he's missing, and his girlfriend was shot in the head. They found her naked in his bedroom."

"Are you sure he was there? You know he leaves her there a lot."

"I know he was there because his clothes and phone were on the floor. Who would do something like this?" She cried and I felt bad. The first person coming to mind is Cat. I instantly called him up.

"What up?" I knew he didn't know who was on the phone because I blocked the number.

"Did you have to kill my grandmother?" I had tears falling down my face. Me and my grandmother were tight.

"Oh hey Wendy. I have no idea what you're talking about. When did she pass?" He was being smart. I could tell by the sarcasm.

"You know when she passed because you did it." I yelled and wiped my face,

"Wendy, I know you're upset about your people passing but don't go around making accusations." He hung up and I received a text from an unknown number.

"YOU'RE NEXT." Is all it read. I dropped my phone, ran in my room and started packing. I know damn well it's him and he must've found that bitch and she told him. But how? Her leg broke when I pushed her in, and Brian buried her in dirt. Nah, she couldn't have survived, could she?

There's really no reason I don't like his bitch Ivy besides she got him to purchase her a damn house and two fucking cars. We were together for a while and he ain't buy me shit. Well he let me stay in his house and all but so what? It's not my fault he pillow talked about having a safe in the house.

Maybe if he had given me money in a bank account and laced me like the new bitch, I wouldn't have had to result in tryna rob him. We tore the house up and the only excuse I could tell him is someone robbed the spot. Who knew he had cameras everywhere? I guess he didn't pillow talk enough or did he mention the safe for a reason. I wonder if it was a setup?

Anyway, his new girl worked as a lawyer and yup I was hating over the fact she had a degree and could buy her own stuff. I don't even know why, when I had a job. It may not pay as much as hers, but I had one. I guess it's true when they say a person can have everything and still wanna take someone else's.

Fuck that tho, Cat owes me for allowing him to do all the freaky shit in the bedroom. Granted, I loved it but he should've paid me for the services. I know ain't no other bitch doing those things. Hell, niggas pay top dollar to be abusive in the bedroom. Its how I make some of my money now. Their fantasies are fulfilled because the women they fuck with ain't having it.

"What you doing?" My sister asked. She and I had a place together. I saw her wiping her eyes which means my mom probably told her.

"Moving." I continued placing things in my duffle bag and suitcase.

"Moving?" She questioned and sat on the bed.

"Yup. I think Cat is gonna kill me."

"For what?" I blew my breath in the air and sat next to her. I loved my sister, but I also know she's gonna go off when I tell her. Its no use in hiding it.

"I been harassing his girl any chance I got and..."

"But why?" My sister ain't confrontational and she hated to hear about me fighting.

"I don't know." She gave me the side eye.

"Fine. Brian and I set it up for his boys to ambush his girls house. They threw smoke bombs inside to distract Cat from her. Brian picked her up and we drove her outta town to a shallow grave." She covered her mouth.

"We threw her in there and I think she broke her ankle. Long story short we buried her alive."

"OH MY GOD WENDY!" She started pacing the room.

"Can you imagine what she was going through?" Is she really worried about the Ivy bitch? I'm her sister and she seem to be more concerned with the bitch I hate.

"Why the fuck you care?"

WHAP! She smacked fire from me. I could've fought her but she had every right to smack me.

"Because you're the reason grandma and Brian are dead. If you left the got damn girl alone this would've never happened."

"How do you know its my fault they died? No one said anything." I hurried to finish packing because of she hits me again, we will fight.

"If you bothered his girl, then I'm sure cat retaliated. What's wrong with you Wendy? Why couldn't you leave him alone?" She started crying again.

"I'm saying. She deserved it." My sister looked at me.

"Really? What did she do to you? Huh? Did she murder anyone? Did she come to your job to fight or anything?" I didn't say anything.

"Exactly. You got us in some bullshit because your ex found someone better. What the fuck?" She stormed out and I could hear her on the phone with someone. I ran down the steps to put my stuff in my car.

"DON'T BRING YOUR ASS BACK HERE." My sister shouted and slammed the door. I sped outta there and made no stops.

****

WHAP! The smack across my face could be heard throughout the repast.

"How dare you bring your ass to my mother's service knowing you brought death to her front door?" My mother had so much venom in her voice it scared me.

"Ma?"

"Ma, my ass. You couldn't leave your ex alone and look what he did." She had tears falling down.

"Get the fuck outta here and I don't wanna see your face again unless it's in a coffin because that's what is gonna happen when he finds you." I felt the eyes on me and didn't move.

"Just go Wendy." My sister grabbed my hand and stepped outside with me.

"You shouldn't have come."

"She's my grandmother too."

"Then why did you put grandma and Brian in a position to lose their life?" I had no answer. I was dead set on making cat suffer I never took in account the way it would affect my family.

"I didn't mean..." She cut me off.

"Now we have no clue if he's gonna come after us to get you."

"Nah, I'm not." Both of us turned and Cat stood there with at least four other dudes.

"See, the reason Brian was taken is because your sister Wendy here, had him punch my fiancé in the face, they kidnapped her, threw her in a ditch and broke her foot." My sister covered her mouth.

"No matter how much she screamed and begged to get out, they ignored her, threw dirt on her and tried to bury her alive." My sister shook her head listening to him recount the shit I did.

"Luckily, my fiancé is strong and pulled herself out. But before she did, she had to stay in the dark, rain with nothing to cover her, and a broken foot, all because this bitch was mad." He mushed me upside the head.

"Is she ok? Cat I'm so sorry she did this." My sister asked with concern. Those two used to joke around a lot when we were together. I know she wasn't asking with bad intent.

"She's gonna have pins and screws in her foot for the rest of her life but it's not gonna stop her from walking down the aisle with me." He smirked after saying it.

"I'm glad to hear it." She told him.

"Tell your mom thanks." I was confused as hell when my sister nodded and left me alone with them. Not one of my family members came to my rescue.

"AHHH." Cat gripped my hair so hard I swore half off it detached from my scalp.

"I should've done this a long time ago." He barked.

BAM! And just like that, he knocked me out.

"Get your stupid ass up." Cat smacked me across the face and drug me out the truck. I tried to run off seeing the exact ditch I pushed Ivy in, but Remi and the other dudes were blocking me.

"Cat, don't do this please." He nudged me to walk closer.

"You see this?" He lifted his shirt.

"This is the spot where the bullet entered because you sent idiots there to kill my girl." I started crying.

"You can thank your mom for filling me in to your whereabouts."

"What?"

"Yea. After I kicked her door down, and put a gun to her head she had no problem telling me when the services were. We all knew you'd be here because you don't know how to stay away." I couldn't believe my mother sold me out.

"I wanna know if all this was worth it?" I went to speak and felt my body being thrown inside the ditch.

"OH MY GOD!" I gasped and covered my mouth staring at Brian's dead corpse. His entire body was topped with dirt up to his neck. His face was blue, and bugs had already begun to eat it.

"I made sure to save space in here for you because after all Wendy, this is what you had planned for my girl. You're gonna feel what it's like to be restrained in a place with minimal movement, bugs eating you and in pain."

POW! He shot me in the foot and I swear half of it came off. He lifted the shovel and tossed more and more dirt on me. He didn't stop until I couldn't move.

"I get it Cat. Please let me go. Your girl made it. Give me a chance to do the same." I pleaded but they fell on deaf ears. I'm not sure how long I screamed and begged for him to let me go but I did hear a voice I never thought I'd hear again.

"How long you gonna be out here?" I looked up and Ivy was sitting on his lap.

"Until she takes her lady breath." He told her.

"That's too long. I need you home in bed with me." He smiled and I hated myself for getting in this position.

"What you wanna do?" She reached in his waist, turned to me, pointed the gun and shot.

"I missed on purpose." She smiled and pointed it again.

"This one won't. Have fun in hell." She pulled the trigger and I closed my eyes thinking it would miss again but nope. I'm dead.

Naima

"Why did you call me over here Mario?" I questioned walking in the house I used to own.

Everything was still the same, but you could see the fire damage my mother did. It wasn't bad enough where you couldn't cook but you saw the black wall over top the stove. The backsplash is gone and so are a lot of other things I kept in here, such as pots hanging over the island, and the color was different. Overall it wasn't the kitchen I left behind, or should I say, the kitchen taken from me.

The living and dining room set is the same and everything in the bathroom remained intact. I didn't want to go in the bedroom because he had sexual relations in the room and there's no need for me to see it.

I did however notice my old clothes in the closet; worn, but there nonetheless. I turned around and he stood there staring at me with his arms folded. As foul as he treated me, nothing could take away how handsome he is.

"I wanted to give you this." He took some papers out his back pocket and walked over to me.

"It better not be you tryna take something..." I cut myself off after noticing the deed with only my name on it.

"But... why would..." My eyes released the water I tried to hold in and suddenly a pair of arms embraced my body.

"I'm sorry for everything Naima. If I could take it back, I would." I continued crying.

"They threatened my kids and I wanted to tell you so many times, but I know you. You wouldn't have wanted me to give in to their demands." I moved him back and stared. What was he referring to and he's right, I would've told him not to do what they say? I have hood people in my family who could've helped.

"Come on. Let me explain." He took my hand in his and something told me to remove mine from his grasp, but I didn't. Sure enough once my feet hit the bottom step, the look on Remi's face said it all. Mario smirked where I probably looked like a deer caught in headlights.

"Am I interrupting?" I let go of Mario's hand.

"No babe. What you doing here?" I moved towards him and leaned on my tippy toes to kiss him. I saw how he kept his eyes on Mario and he should've because it's no telling what he's up to.

"You ok? Is Ivy ok?" I glanced over at Cat who stared at this African painting I purchased when I first brought this house.

"She good. Her mom is there driving her crazy but she a'ight. Yo, where you get this?" Cat answered still glancing at the photo.

"What's really going on Mario? Why you call my girl over here?" I never got the chance to respond to Cat because my new man demanded answers from my old one.

"Oh, you told him?" Mario questioned as if him asking me to stop by should be a secret.

"Ugh Yea. He's my man and I'm supposed to tell him when my ex contacts me out the blue after stripping my home away." I stood in front of Remi hoping he'd stay calm.

"What you want?" Remi questioned him again.

"He gave me back my house babe and was bringing me down here to talk."

"Talk huh? What kind of talking requires holding your hand?" Remi was aggravated and I didn't want him fighting. I took his hand in mine because sometimes it calms him.

"Look, I don't want no problems. I just came to give her house back and tell her to be careful." Remi flew from around me and hemmed Mario up so fast Cat couldn't stop him if he wanted to.

"You play too many games. Tell my girl what you need to and take your punk ass the fuck outta here." Mario turned to me.

"Don't look at her. If she gave a fuck about you this wouldn't be happening." I left them standing there and picked the couch pillows up and tossed them out the door.

"What you doing Naima?" Cat asked. Remi still had Mario against the wall.

"He gave me my house back but it's no way in hell I'm keeping anything. The kitchen has to be re done, I have to hire painters and it's so much to do, I need to get started."

BOOM! I heard and turned in the direction of Remi. Mario was on the ground and my man had his foot on his chest. I shook my head.

"Don't worry about fixing anything." Remi said.

"Babe, he had his ex living here and..."

"And you're my woman. I'm gonna have people in here tomorrow to get an estimate on what needs to be done." I walked over to him.

"I'm gonna need to compensate you for your generosity." I smirked when I said it.

"Trust, there's a way for you to compensate. Remember the..."

"Hell fucking no! Y'all not about to discuss things you do in the bedroom." Cat shouted and we started laughing.

"Umm, you think your foot can be lifted off his chest so he can tell me what's going on?" We both stared down at Mario who sucked his teeth. Remi moved his foot and stepped away.

"What's going Mario?" I stood there waiting for him to stand.

"First off... keep that psychotic nigga away from me."

He spoke in a soft tone and wiped his clothes off.

"Who Remi? He's a big teddy bear." He gave me a look.

"Ok maybe he is to me." I shrugged my shoulders.

"Anyway, these people sent me to your mother's house to tear walls down for a safe."

"That was you?" I became aggravated and raised my voice a little, which made Remi come over. Not that he was far, but he gave us space. I told him what Mario said and he cut his eyes at him. If I weren't here there's no doubt in my mind Remi would do a lot more.

"They wanted the things in the safe but the only things in there were papers, a picture and DVD. What they were looking for, wasn't." I thought about telling him my mother had it but Remi's eyes spoke to me silently and said keep my mouth closed. I have relatives in the streets, so I know a little something about not volunteering information.

"Who are these people?" Remi asked and at first Mario was hesitant to answer.

"My ex Lina is related to them."

"Ex?" I questioned because when he kicked me out you would've thought they were about to get married.

"Yea. Unfortunately, they killed her because she contacted the police when I was at your moms."

"Why would she do that?" Cat asked coming closer.

"I hung up on her."

"That's dumb." Remi told him and I agreed. I don't know why she called in the process of him looking when she knew it was for, but she's always been spiteful. He should've known she'd do something stupid.

"It is. The guys were pissed because she could've gotten me caught and they wouldn't have retrieved the item from me, which they didn't anyway." He blew his breath in the air.

"Long story short, whatever they're looking for, they won't stop until they find it; even if it means hurting you to get it." My body stiffened up.

"You don't have a name? What do they look like?" Remi began bombarding him with tons of questions.

131

"I did what they asked and right now my kids are safe. It doesn't mean they're not coming up with another plan to get you."

"Remi." I felt him directly behind me.

"Next time they call, if they do, give them my phone number." Mario chuckled.

"They know who you are."

"WHAT?" I shouted.

"He told me about how overprotective he is of you and he's one of the reasons they haven't been able to touch you. Well him and others." I was nervous as hell and Remi knew it.

He had Cat walk me outside and shockingly he stayed in to converse with Mario. I just knew my man was going to kill him, instead they stepped out the house and spoke about linking up later.

"Take my truck to the house Cat. I'm gonna drive her home." He nodded and after Mario left so did Cat. We sat there for a few minutes.

"Soooo, the house was tapped prior to him throwing you out." I snapped my neck

"Naima, I don't know what our fathers were into, but it seems like this person is from their past." I heard everything he said but all I could think of is how he said my house was recorded. How did they get in? Were they tapping my new house? My phone?

"Come over here Naima." He pushed the seat back as far as it could go and had me place my knees on the side of him. I thought we were about to have sex because he pulled my pants and panties down.

"Relax ma. Ain't nobody here." I nodded and placed my hand on top of his head when he put his mouth on my clit. Ever since the first time he went down, it's like he had to do it.

"Yes Remi. Right there baby." His face was damn near inside my pussy.

"Mmm. Shit baby." I came on his face and instantly felt my body relax. He started unbuckling his jeans and I figured it's only fair to return the favor, but he thought otherwise and had me sit down.

"You feel good ma." His hands went up and down my back as I moved my hips in circles. He lifted my shirt, and bra with unhooking it and began sucking on my breast. The feeling became intense and the two of us got lost in each other.

"I never knew a woman could make me feel this good." He yanked my hair back and thrusted under me. The car was rocking, and I kept hitting the horn; yet neither of us cared to stop.

"Let me put my son in you." I couldn't respond because my eyes were now rolling, and the climax was right there.

"I don't hear you Naima. Can I put my kid in you?" He thrusted harder and I sunk my nails deep in his shoulders.

"Say it."

"Remi, you sure we're ready?" I managed to get out.

"Yup. Fuck I'm about to cum. Let me know what you wanna do." I felt his dick twitching inside.

"I love you so much baby." I said and crashed my mouth on his. There were no words left to be said as we moaned in each other's mouth at the same time we released. Both of us were breathing fast. I rested my head on his shoulder.

"I love you too." He said and reached over to grab some napkins out the glove compartment. He cleaned both of us the best he could and helped me put my clothes on.

"You know our parents are gonna be a pain in the ass when you do get pregnant." He and I shared a laugh.

"As long as you're by my side, I don't care." I told him.

"I'm not going nowhere." I moved into my own seat.

"Baby what's that?" I pointed to what appeared to be the figure of a person.

"Probably someone walking by."

"I hope it's someone walking by and they didn't see us."

"They probably didn't because you fogged the windows up with all that moaning." I busted out laughing. Remi pulled off and drove straight to his house. He hated staying in my condo. Talking about it's too small and not what he's used to.

****

"Oh shit bitch. This nigga putting kids in you?" Ivy all but shouted. I was at her house because the guys were at

Remi's parents discussing whatever Mario said when I walked away.

"I don't know if he did yet."

"If he let loose in you, unless one of y'all sterile, he put a damn baby in you." I laid on the loveseat.

"It hasn't been long enough Ivy and..."

"And shut up. You wanted a kid with Mario before he messed up." I waved her off. I just knew Mario and I would be married but it looks like that wasn't in our plans.

"I'm serious Naima. I don't think you loved your ex the same way you love Remi." I sat up.

"What you mean?"

"You and Remi are on an entirely different level mentally. You both have money, work your asses off and don't need one another for anything. It may only be a year but fuck it. He asked you so he knows you're not tryna trap him."

"I know." I let my hand slide through my hair.

"Ma is gonna be so happy and I'm the first godmother. Margie better beat it." She said and Margie gave her the finger. She was in the bathroom but knew about Remi asking me too.

136

"Whatever y'all do, I'm supporting." Margie said and took a seat.

"You talking about me, when is the wedding?" I asked Ivy.

"When I can walk again heffa." We all looked at her foot.

The day Remi found her, they had to do emergency surgery. Her foot was so bad they thought they'd have to amputate it. Luckily, they didn't because she would've been a mess.

Anyway, she had to get screws and pins in it and has this cast on for the next month or two. She complains a lot and I understand but Cat tells her to be quiet because she's alive and it's all that mattered. He'll marry her on the couch if it's what Ivy wanted. She can pop all the shit she wants but her ass works from home and they have sex. Ivy be talking just to be talking sometimes.

Remi

"It sounds like Julio is in town and he's going to stop at nothing until he gets the ring." My pops said sitting at the table with me and Cat.

After leaving Naima over Ivy's, I thought it was best to discuss these people coming for her and her mother. Who knew my family had this much affiliation with hers? My father was right about one thing and that's, that Naima got my ass in love and no one is gonna fuck with her.

When I mentioned to Naima, I didn't know a woman could make me feel that good, I wasn't lying. All the years of touring different countries, in and outta women's beds and not giving a fuck never bothered me. Now here I have a woman I'm actually claiming, fell in love with her and can't see myself without her. And then the sex is on another level because the love and feelings are there. I keep saying who knew, but my pops did. He knew some chick would have me wide open. I'm happy it's someone who feels the same because I'd hate to murk a bitch for tryna play me.

Anyway, Mario mentioned these guys are after Naima and her mom. I decided not to bring up the ring as the item they're searching for to see if he knew anything. It's unfortunate I almost had to beat his ass, but I respected him for informing my girl. He could've kept it to himself.

It bothered me a little to see him holding her hand and even more to witness the fire he still had burning for her. I know she doesn't want him, and I have no doubt he did what he had to for his kids. I would've done the same.

In the process, Mario lost the woman he claimed to love and almost his life. The least I could do is give some sort of assistance because he did get Naima away safely; even if it was in a fucked up way. His fuck up led her in my direction, and it allowed me to experience love for the first time.

And no, I don't and never had these feelings towards Nelly. She was just a girl I slept with, who slept with my brother, continued sleeping with him and tried to screw me anytime she saw me. The two of us would've never worked out because I'd probably choke the shit outta her. As far as Monee, boy do I have plans for her.

"Where does this Julio guy live?" I asked at the same time my mom stepped in the kitchen. My father's eyes lit up and she blushed. Those two are probably still in the newlywed stage. No wonder Ivan left. I'm sure they're making up for lost time.

"I have people looking for him and so does Nyeemah's people."

"And who are they?" Cat asked.

"The Carters over there in the Marcus Garvey projects."

"Oh shit really?" I was shocked because we knew everyone over there.

"Yea and trust they're very aware of you and her relationship." I gave him the side eye.

"You may not know but their family is very close. Never mind Nyeemah went there as soon as she saw me."

"Oh they got beef?" Me and Cat questioned at the same time.

"No. They cussed my ass out for not telling them I was home tho. Honestly, they're cool as hell." We nodded.

KNOCK! KNOCK! I walked in the other room to answer the door. I opened it and this bitch had the nerve to bite down on her lip as if I'd ever give her dirty ass a chance.

"Tha fuck you want Nelly?"

"You but you're acting stingy with the dick."

"Nah. My girl stingy with my dick."

"Oh the bitch who let your brother feel all over her and when she thought someone peeped it, she ran upstairs? You mean her?" She had a grin on her face.

"I'm not even gonna entertain the nonsense Ivan told you because it's no need. I will say, rent is due in two days and if y'all ain't got it, guess who getting put the fuck out?" Her mouth dropped.

"I'm not the type of landlord who's gonna put up with late rent."

"How are you the landlord when my name is on the paperwork? I mean..."

"Let me stop you right there stupid." I put my hand up.

"Stupid?" She shouted.

141

"Yea stupid. He told you your name was on the paperwork, correct?" She didn't answer.

"His name was actually on it dummy. Second... any money my brother uses has to be approved through me because I'm the sole provider of his estate." Her mouth dropped.

"So you see, even though he had you believing the place is yours, the money funding it came from an account I set up linked to me."

"What?"

"I may not have known about it right away because I have a real job and my accountant deals with his stupidity. Therefore; he just relinquished the money with no questions asked. Oh but be reassured his ass is gone as well so no free money coming your way." She was pissed but not as much as I was learning Ivan had been doing stupid stuff for a long time now. Outta all the things he should've done, one would think he'd start a business but nope. All he worried about was spending.

"Now that we're clear on those issues, why the fuck you here?" I folded my arms across my chest and waited for he to answer.

"Here you go." My pops spoke behind me. I turned and saw a big box in his hand and my mom had some more bags.

"Can you help me put those in my car?" She asked.

"Hell no!" My pops responded and shocked me.

"Excuse me!"

"You're excused."

"Why are you mad at me?" My father looked her up and down.

"Because you're a whore who slept with both of my sons. Over the years, you continued sleeping with the one you assumed had the most money, only to try and fuck the one you shitted on all those years ago every time you see him." She stood there silent.

"Let's not forget, once you found out Remi's the one with the money, you threw that raunchy, fishy coochie at him but he's not weak like my other son." My mom tried to intervene.

"You should've told your fake ass man to come get his own shit." My father tossed the box on the ground, took the other stuff from my mother and did the same. I had no idea why they were doing that but with Ivan you never know.

"He doesn't listen to me." She said and picked up the bags she could carry. I could be a gentleman and help but I'll pass.

"Don't forget, rent is due in two days." I shut the door and followed my parents in the house to find out what's going on. For them to throw his stuff it only means something happened.

"Why you throw his stuff pops?" I asked plopping down next to him on the couch.

"Your mother asked me not to mention it." I glanced over at her.

"It's not a big deal Remi. We handled it and..." My father stormed out the living room.

"That don't look handled." My mother took a seat next to me.

"Ivan has some issues." I scoffed up a laugh.

144

"I'm serious. He's become very hateful, jealous and violent." I jumped off the couch.

"Did he put his hands on you?" She stood.

"No Remi."

"Tell him the truth." My father leaned against the wall drinking a soda, while Cat waited for my mom to speak too.

"He was upset that you have a lot and..."

"And the nigga tried it with your mother, she punched him in the face, I tried to kill him and now he's gone." My mother gave him a nasty glare.

"Be mad all you want. I may have been locked down all those years, but both of my sons were taught respect and to never raise a hand to their mother. I swear if you weren't here, I probably would've killed him." My father spoke with a ton of venom in his voice.

"WHAT?"

"Remi please. I don't need my sons fighting and it's over. He's gone, my husband's home, and you're doing great in life. I just want some peace right now." She fell back on the couch. Cat looked at me.

"Please leave it alone." My eyes met my fathers and I could see the aggravation in his.

"Ma, this ain't ok." She had her head in her hands.

"When am I getting grandkids?" She smiled, which made me do the same. As angry as I was about Ivan, I couldn't help but let it go for now.

"Who knows? Lately I ain't been pulling out." She popped me on the shoulder.

"What?

"I love you all." She kissed me and Cat's cheek and told my father she was going upstairs to lie down. All of us stared and remained quiet. We heard the door close and I grabbed my keys.

"Let it go for now Remi." I stopped at the door when my father said it.

"Pops."

"I know son and I would love nothing more for you to beat his ass. However, we both know he's a got damn snitch and will tell your mother quick. I'll be damned if she holds out on pussy." My face turned up.

"I've been gone too long for her to be selfish." We all busted out laughing.

"One more time pops and ma just going be mad."

"I agree." We said our goodbyes.

"He on some other shit." Cat said when we sat in the truck.

"I know. I hate to say it, but my brother is gonna make me kill him." I pulled off thinking about how I'm going to do it.

****

"What's going on here?" I stepped in Club Turquoise this morning to drop some papers off and there were a bunch of cars in front of it. It was a few cops, and the health inspector Margie, who's friends with Naima was here. I peeped her lawyer, along with mine who had a smirk on his face which usually meant he's about to sue or he knows something and waiting for the right time to say it. I wasn't worried because all my shit legit. Naima pulled up behind my truck looking as lost as me.

"What's going on?" She ran over to me.

"I was about to ask the same question. How did you know?" Margie raised her hand.

"Mr. Stevens, we have reason to believe the woman standing next to you passed your inspection due to the intimate relationship you two have." Some guy who introduced himself as the lead supervisor at the fire station said. Right then, I knew this had Victoria written all over it.

"Where did you hear that?"

"I'm not at liberty to reveal that information."

"Well if the person informed you of that would you like to step inside and do a check for yourself?" I unlocked the door and all of us went in.

"Let me assure you that Ms. Carter and I had no affiliation at the time of the inspection." He stopped looking down at his clipboard and up at me.

"Actually, I was outta town and my brother Ivan Stevens is the individual who opened the doors for Ms. Carter to inspect this place, in which she failed by the way." His entire demeanor changed.

"Excuse me." He said.

"Exactly. Ms. Carter closed the place until further notice. I had to contact my lawyer and take the case to court to get it re-opened. The judge had another inspector who you see standing over there re-inspect the place." He was turning red by the minute.

"After the small fire took place here not too long ago, your employer Victoria stopped by to give me a full report among other things." Just as I mentioned her, she walked in smiling.

"Other things?" He questioned and I turned to look at Victoria who had no clue as to what was going on.

"Oh yes. Your employer offered to suck my dick and fuck me in my office." His facial expression was funny.

"When my woman stopped by and caught her, she made threats about making up stories to say Ms. Carter was the help and it's the only reason Club Turquoise passed. Isn't that right?" Victoria couldn't pick her mouth up fast enough.

"When the kitchen was fixed, a different inspector came in and passed it. Naima nor her boss Margie had any affiliation with the handling of that inspection." The guy from the fire station had no words.

"Feel free to check for yourself again." He stepped away and went to do his own check.

"You thought this would end in your favor Victoria but I'm a smart, hood nigga. I've been ten steps ahead of you the whole time." I moved closer to her.

"You got one more time to try some dumb shit and you won't be alive long enough to do another inspection in hopes to get fucked."

"Remington..." Naima moved me away from her.

"Get the fuck out before I beat your ass." She stormed passed us and pushed the door open hard.

The guy didn't stay long at all and apologized for his employee. He claims there shouldn't be any more issues from her moving forward. Once everyone left, Naima and I were in the office talking.

"You sound sexy as hell talking professionally. And before you say it, I'm not saying anything bad." She sat on my lap facing me.

"It was sexy huh?" She placed soft kisses on my neck.

"Hell yea."

"I think you should offer up an award for it."

"An award?" She smirked and stood to take her clothes off.

"It better be worth it because you know I don't usually do office sex."

"Oh, don't you worry Remington Stevens III. It's gonna be well worth it." She winked and all I can say is, she didn't lie.

Ivan

"Your rude ass father damn near bit my head off when he saw me. Then, he threw the suitcase and bags on the ground and told me hell no he wasn't helping me put them in the car. And that was after he told me off and called me a whore." Nelly explained in detail the things that took place when she stopped by my parents.

I could've gone myself but then we would've been arguing and I'm over them. Plus, my brother was there and if he found out what I did and said to my mother, it's no doubt in my mind he'd kill me. He's always been the baby outta us and regardless of the money he gave me, it doesn't make him better.

"Then, Remi said you had two days to have the rent or we getting kicked out. Ivan what's going on because I was under the assumption you had money."

"I do." I lifted my beer to drink.

"He says you don't and the accountant who handled your affairs has been terminated." She revealed new information to me because no one told me.

I mean yea, Remi has always been in charge of the money he dispensed to me, but his accountant never questioned what it was needed for. If he fired him it means I can't do what I want with the remaining money I have, unless Remi approves it.

"Nelly did you really stick around for the money?" I don't know what made me ask.

"Ivan, you of all people should know the answer to your own question." She rose up off the couch and I grabbed her wrist.

"If I did, I wouldn't ask." She sat back down and looked at me.

"Ivan we've been sleeping with each other off and on for years. You've been with other woman and I've been with other men. You've funded my lifestyle and I appreciate it but if you're broke, I have to move on." I nodded my head.

"Do you regret choosing me over Remi?"

"Actually yes. Remi was good to me as a friend before we even slept together. I only wanted to be with an older guy because my friends were. Then you taught me things in the bedroom and started giving me money. I wasn't gonna pass up anything; especially, when you offered without me asking."

"I see." I didn't know if I should be mad or respect her hustle.

"I've experienced other men and sadly, in the beginning I couldn't handle how big they were after being with you for so long."

"What the fuck you tryna say?"

"Ivan don't play as if you don't know your dick is below average size." She rolled her eyes.

"Why continue sleeping with me then?"

"I just told you. The money kept me here and I'm not saying the sex is bad. I'm saying after being with others I noticed the difference."

"All these years my family said you were using me, and I didn't listen."

"You should've. Most people can tell." She shrugged her shoulders.

"Ok." I said and put my beer on the coffee table.

We're not in love or anything like that but I did believe

she had some feelings for me. I mean damn! We've been

together all these years and I'm just learning it was for the

money. Maybe, I was in denial but whatever the case, she

fucked with the wrong dude and today is gonna be her first

lesson. Never fuck with a person's feelings or stick around

with for the wrong reasons.

WHAP! WHAP! I smacked her over and over.

"IVAN STOP!" She started kicking at me and I moved

each time.

"Get out!" I grabbed her hair and literally drug her out

the house.

I opened the door and she began to scream. I pulled her

back in, stomped on her face a few times and continued

kicking her again. The screaming stopped, which made me

look and Nelly appeared to be dead.

I went upstairs, changed my shoes because there was

blood on them and left the house with her inside. The bitch

thought she had one up on me. I bet she doesn't anymore.

****

155

"Is your husband home?" I asked my mother on the phone. She's been asking me to stop by so we could talk about what happened.

"No. Are you here?" I noticed the shade go up in the living room and soon the door opened. I stepped out my car and surveyed the area to be sure my father or Remi wasn't pulling up.

"Hey Ivan. I missed you so much." She hugged me and it was pure torture to return the embrace. I loved my mother, but I also know where her allegiance lies and it ain't with me.

"Do you have anything to eat?" I moved passed and walked straight in the kitchen.

"There's some meatloaf in there and the sides are in Tupperware." I grabbed a plate from the cabinet and began opening the different containers to make me a plate.

"Ivan, I want to talk to you about…"

"DAMN MA. CAN I MAKE MY FUCKING PLATE FIRST?" I shouted making her jump. She put her hands up in surrender. I placed my food in the microwave and turned around.

"Not so tough when your husband isn't here."

"Son, I don't wanna fight with you. I'll wait for you to finish." She took a seat at the table after making a cup of coffee.

BEEP! BEEP! The microwave went off. I removed my plate, grabbed some silverware and sat down. Remembering I had nothing to drink, I hopped up and took a soda out. My mother stared at me with concern, sadness and disappointment on her face. It angered me and I snapped.

"What the fuck are you looking at?" I started antagonizing her because no one was here. I wanted to see if she'd pop off at the mouth like before when my father was home.

"What do you want Ivan? Is it money? Is it attention? Just tell me so I can make you happy. I hate this distance and bad energy surrounding this family." I ignored her.

"IVAN STEVENS! DON'T YOU DARE IGNORE ME."

"Or what?" I looked up at her.

"Or what huh?" I dropped my fork and pushed my chair out.

"You know what? This was a bad idea and it's time for you to go." We were both standing, and I give it to my mother, she refused to back down.

"I'm not going anywhere. You offered me food and I'm gonna finish it." I went to sit back down and felt hot liquid going down the back of my neck.

"What the fuck?"

"Get outta my house." She had her arms folded and it pissed me off to see she wasn't worried about anything. I walked towards her and she moved back.

WHAP! I backhanded the shit outta her. The force swung her body around and she caught herself from falling by gripping the countertop.

"That's for the last time you put your hands on me. Whew! It felt good too." I shook my neck and jumped up and down.

"You wanna fight? Ok." She used her thumb to clean the blood leaking from her lip.

"Ahhhhh." I never saw her leg lift but her kick to the balls was on point. I dropped to my knees giving her full access to do whatever.

"I told you before, my sons will respect me."

WHAP! She smacked and punched me over and over. I couldn't even stop her because my dick was in a lotta pain.

"Now. Like I said, get the fuck…" She tried to say. I mustered up enough energy to grab her leg. She hit the ground and her other foot was kicking me in the face, but I still didn't let go.

"Let me go." She tried to release herself from me. I was finally able to get up and lifted her by the hair.

"I'm going to have to beat your ass the same way I did Nelly." I banged her face into the wall on the way out the kitchen and heard her nose crack or break.

"You think because you're my mother, I'm supposed to be ok with the way you speak or put your hands on me? Nah. I'm not built that way." I continued dragging her up the steps by the hair, with her nose bleeding and her screaming.

"Get me the money out your safe." I tossed her on the floor in her bedroom. She held her nose and pressed her back against the bed.

"Ok fine. What's the combination?" Her crying started getting on my nerves.

"SHUT THAT FUCKING CRYING UP!" I yelled in her face and demanded the combination again. I was aggravated when she said it was my birthday. That's dumb; especially since she hates me.

The safe opened and there had to be at least a million dollars in it. I grabbed a duffle bag from the side of the closet and placed all of it inside. I closed it back and stared at my mother lying in a fetal position in front of the bed.

"Let's get this over with." She looked at me with fear. Blood still gushing out and her face was turning pale.

"It has to appear to be a break in and then an accident." I shrugged and drug her by the feet out the room.

"NO IVAN. LET GO!" She shouted and it fell on deaf ears. Her hands were grasping at the rails of the steps.

"Don't worry. The fall won't be too hard."

"What?"

"When you die, I'm sure your insurance policy will pay me a lot."

"Ivan please don't do this."

"You have to die because if not, you'll tell that husband and son of yours. They'll kill me and I can't have that. I'm just getting started."

"Please Ivan." Her begging started getting on my nerves.

"No need to beg and you're dying anyway. I mean look at all the blood on the ground. Why delay the inevitable?" The look on her face was priceless. Now she'll see how it feels when someone has you at a disadvantage like my father did when he choked me, or the many times Remi beat my ass.

"And down goes Frazier." I laid her in front of the steps and used my foot to push her. I watched her body roll down the hard-wooden stairs and smiled. It had to hurt and once she hit bottom and didn't move, I felt my job here was done.

I reached the bottom of the steps and kneeled down. Unfortunately, she wasn't dead but by the shallow breaths she took, I knew her time was coming. I kneeled down next to her and lifted her head.

"I told you to leave me the fuck alone. You should've never allowed me back in the same house you kicked me out of dumb bitch."

BAM! I slammed her face into the ground. There was no sound which again, led me to believe she's on her way out. All I have to do is wait for the call and cash in my policy. Life is good.

Naima

"Wow! It came out so nice." I gushed to Remi about the kitchen in my house.

It's been three weeks since Mario returned it and it didn't resemble anything like before. The floors were all different, the paint color changed in every room and the kitchen is like one out of a magazine. Remi even had the back deck re-done and added a BBQ pit. It made me think freaky sex isn't anywhere near enough to compensate for the money he most likely put out.

"You must be crazy if you thought I'd leave remnants of any man in here. Yo ass won't be reminiscing about anyone except me." He had me against the wall with his hand over my head.

"Remi this is nice and way too much money. Let me give you some back."

"No need. If you're pregnant that's more than enough payment." He rubbed my belly.

"And if I'm not?"

"Then you'll be compensating until you are." I snickered and placed a kiss on his lips.

"You hungry?" He asked after we took one last look at the place. The furniture was being delivered this weekend and I couldn't wait to stay here.

My mom decided to keep the condo and sale the house Mario broke in. She's excited to be somewhere she's not responsible for fixing anything or snow removal. She's far from lazy and has a new man but will tell you in a minute, she ain't built for hard labor unless it's beating someone's ass.

"Yea. I think Paradise sounds good." I told him as he locked the door. I loved that place and his chef always made me the best food. It does help when you're sleeping with the boss tho.

He parked in his spot and walked around the truck to help me out. We were far from dressed up and this place required business or dressy attire. He told me not to worry about it but when we stepped in and everyone looked nice, and I felt uncomfortable. He held my hand and took us to a table in the corner where no one could see anything. I loved this spot and a few times we did inappropriate things here.

"Look who decided to grace us with their presence." Tara sassed and scooted me over.

"Can't you see me and my baby mama tryna have dinner?"

"OH MY GOD! YOU PREGNANT?" She asked excitedly and started feeling my stomach.

"Not yet but it doesn't stop him from trying."

"Hell no and when she gets pregnant, I'm still not pulling out." Tara threw a napkin at him.

"Anyway. My aunt told me about your house being renovated. Don't forget a sister when you throwing BBQ's."

"Never that."

"Damn Tara. It's too early to be inviting yourself to our house." I smiled and didn't even correct him. He considered his place mine so why wouldn't I do the same?

"There you are." We all turned our heads and Monee was standing there outta breath and holding her chest.

"Bitch, if you don't get your dirty ass from over here, I'm gonna beat your face in." I tried to be as calm as possible because if I am expecting, I didn't wanna have a miscarriage from fighting.

"Hold on." This bitch was really testing me, and Remi must've had enough because he pushed Monee back making her hit the floor.

"WAIT! PLEASE. I'M TRYING TO TELL YOU SOMETHING BAD HAPPENED TO YOUR MOTHER." Remi snatched her up off the ground.

"What the fuck you talking about?"

"Babe, she can't speak because you're choking her." I had to make him release her. She hit the floor hard.

"What happened to his mom?" I had to get down to Monee's level because the longer she took to speak, the angrier he was. Tara had a few bouncers come over to hold him.

"I went to the house his brother had and the door was unlocked. His girlfriend was on the ground damn near beat to death. When the EMT's arrived, the cops asked if she knew who did it and she blamed Ivan."

"BITCH YOU SAID MY MOTHER." Remi shouted.

"I rode by his mother's place and there were cops and ambulances there too." Just as she finished telling me, Remi's phone rang and so did Tara's.

"WHAT? WHERE ARE YOU?" I stood in front of Remi.

"Let's go."

"Is she ok?" I asked grabbing my things and running behind her.

"I don't know. My father said she's at the hospital and they don't know if she's going to make it." I saw a few tears falling down his face and snatched the keys out his hand.

"I'll drive." He jumped in the passenger side and we heard the back door open. Tara hopped in the back seat.

"She's gonna be ok Remi." Tara said rubbing his shoulders. I remained quiet because I didn't know what to say.

I grabbed his hand and held the whole way there. I dropped him off at the emergency room door and told them I'd be right in. Remi was very hesitant to allow me outta his sight until Tara reminded him cops were here. He kissed me and said hurry up parking the truck.

I found a parking spot, pulled in and grabbed my purse. As I walked in my mother called. I answered and explained what all Monee told us. My mother couldn't believe it and said she was on her way. After she told me the truth about my father, I introduced her, and Remi and they got along great.

My foot was at the threshold of the door when someone yanked me back and put their hand over my mouth. I started kicking and tried to bite whoever it was.

"It took me forever to get you." I froze.

The person whispering in my ear was the same one who entered my hospital room. He had the familiar smell of liquor and even though he spoke softly, I knew it was him. The tears flowed instantly and even though I could see Remi and his family through the glass, none of them were facing my direction.

"Yo, what you doing?" I heard Mario's voice and did everything I could to break free. This person had a death grip on me. What is he doing here anyway?

"Let her go." Mario ran up and someone came out the shadows and dug a knife in his back.

"AHHHH." He shouted and fell to the ground.

"Help me get her in the van before they notice." All the muffled screaming, kicking and scratching did nothing to help set me free.

BOOM! They tossed me in the van, and I felt a blow to my back. It was so hard, I had to be paralyzed.

"What the fuck? A baseball bat?" The person pulled whoever was with him to the side.

"Yup. Her head is next." This is not how I expected to die.

Cat

"Are you sure this is the house she picked?" I asked my mom.

Ivy finally picked a date she wanted to get married on and one of her gifts was a brand-new house. She loved the other one I purchased but now the memories are too bad. We could stay at my place, but she wanted something bigger due to all the kids she wanted. It's funny because men are usually the ones who want all the bad ass boys running around.

"I'm positive." She had a huge grin on her face.

"Ok. We'll take it." I told the realtor. Now she had a huge grin on her face, and she should. Not only am I paying cash for this spot, her cut is gonna be nice.

The house sat on three acres, had six bedrooms, a basketball court out back, a pool, three car garage and it was fenced in the front and back. Ivy always mentioned tryna learn how to plant flowers and shit. This place is huge so she can plant every tree or flower in the world.

"She's going to be so happy." I filled out all the paperwork and the lady said she'll contact me with a closing date.

"Now let's get her new car."

"Ma, she just got a brand new one last year."

"Exactly! Last year. If you're gonna upgrade, you may as well go all out." I shook my head because she doing the most.

We drove to the Mercedes lot and just like I expected, the sales people rushed over. My mother told them to back up and if we needed them, she'd say something. I couldn't do shit but laugh because they all seemed shocked a woman pushed them away.

"Hey sexy." I answered for Ivy.

"Soooooo I was thinking that next week is a good time to set up a prenatal appointment. I mean we shouldn't wait to..."

"WHAT?" I stopped walking.

"You did it baby."

"Did what?" I knew what she was talking about but wanted to hear her say it.

"We're having a baby." The shit had me smiling from ear to ear.

I wanted her to have my child since the first time we slept together. I understood why she decided to wait and honestly after the things we've been through I'm glad we did. I can't begin to think about what would've happened if our kid was at the house when Wendy and her cousin attacked. The shit makes me mad each time I think about it.

"Are you happy?" Ivy asked and I couldn't stop smiling.

"This is it." My mother spoke softly and pointed to a silver 2019 Mercedes GLC truck.

"Hell yea I'm happy. You know I've been tryna get you pregnant forever." She laughed in the phone.

"Hurry home so I can thank you."

"A'ight but it's gonna have to wait because your mother in law said she staying over."

"It's ok. We got all night."

172

BEEP! I took the phone from my ear to see who was calling.

"I'll see you when I get there. Remi on the other line."

"Ok tell him to have Naima call me. I've been tryna reach her."

"A'ight."

"Yo!" I clicked over.

"Bro I need you at the hospital." I don't know why but my heart started beating fast.

"You good?"

"Something happened to ma and I can't find Naima. One minute she was parking the truck and the next she went missing. Shit is all fucked up."

"I'll be right there." I hung up and told my mother we'd have to come another day.

"What's going on?"

"I don't know. Remi called and some shit went down with his mom. He can't find Naima and she went there with him." She gasped.

"We should pick Ivy up."

"Nah because she'll worry, and I can't have her losing my baby."

"SHE'S PREGNANT? OH MY GOD!" She was jumping up and down in the seat.

"Calm down ma. We can't go inside being happy when they're going through something."

"Ok. Ok. I hope both of them are ok." It took twenty minutes to get there. My phone rang and it was Ivy again. I wonder if Remi contacted her too.

"Cat, I need you." I stopped walking in the middle of the parking lot.

"What's wrong? Are you ok?" Her voice was trembling, and I could tell she was most likely shaking.

"Baby, they're taking me to jail for murder."

"For what? I know it's not Wendy?" I know damn well we did a good job covering our tracks for her.

"No, it's not for her or the cousin." She whispered as low as she could.

"Then what the fuck they taking you to jail for?"

"Remi's mother. They're saying its attempted murder now but if she dies, its first degree." All the air left my body. This couldn't be happening.

"Ma'am that's enough time. You have the right to remain silent..." I heard an officer in the background right before the phone went dead.

Remi

"Tell me Naima is outside." I rushed over to Cat's mom. She seemed to be shaken up and her eyes were watery.

"Where's Cat?" I peeked around her in search of my boy.

"Remi, Ivy called when we pulled in and said she was being arrested." She placed her hand on the side of my face.

"Arrested? For what?" She swallowed hard.

"For whatever happened to your mom."

"SAY WHAT?" I was about to speak when I noticed Nyeemah's mom step in the hospital. My phone went off at the same time. I spoke and told her to give me a minute.

"Who this?" I never bothered to look at the number because not only was Ivy arrested for my mother, here was Naima's searching the waiting room for her daughter.

"Remington Stevens III." The man speaking my full name on the phone had my attention.

"It's a lot going on tonight, isn't it?" I glanced around the waiting room myself and no one had a phone to their ear.

"Who the fuck is this?"

"Tsk, Tsk, Tsk. Is that the way you speak to the man who holds your future in his hands?" I chuckled.

"This must be Julio." Now it was his turn to laugh.

"Correct."

"What you want and how the fuck you holding my future in your hands?"

"It seems Naima is missing; your mother suffered some pain this evening and your brother is beating up old girlfriends of yours. The way I see it is, you can't possibly run businesses when your name is attached to scandals."

"Nigga shut the fuck up. What you calling me for?" I wasn't about to go back and forth with this nigga.

"All I want is what's been taking from me years ago." He said smugly in the phone.

"You watching my girl over a damn ring?"

"Ahh. So you know what I want? Your father must've filled you in."

"Look. This shit is childish as fuck right now. We'll deal with you another time." I hung up on him and walked over to my pops who looked stressed out.

"I've been in jail for years Remi and all I thought about the entire time is coming home to my family. I can't lose my wife, son." It's like the entire emergency room went silent.

"Pops she's not gonna die."

"You didn't see her. Blood was everywhere and she was barely breathing."

"How did you know?" I asked because my father was at my office counting money for me. I've been running around doing other things and with the accountant gone, I had to make sure my money was on point until I found another one.

"I don't know how she did it, but your mom called me and said to hurry home. I didn't even bother asking what happened and called the cops myself. I flew home and when I got there the cops and ambulance were pulling up at the same time."

"Was anyone there with her?" I wanted to know if a neighbor saw what happened or if they saw Ivy leaving.

"No one was with her and that's what's fucking me up. She laid there dying and I don't even know if she had any idea I was there. Son she was..." He stopped speaking and wiped his eyes.

"Have you looked at the cameras in the house yet?" He shook his head no.

"I can't right now. I don't wanna see what went down until I know she's ok." I sat next to him.

"The nigga called requesting his ring." My father looked at me. I had to change the subject because he was making me more upset.

"Talking about he knows everything going on within the family."

"I'm not surprised." I blew my breath and sat back. I had to tell him about my girl.

"Naima's missing and they've arrested Ivy for ma."

"What?" My phone rang again. This time I looked hoping it was Naima, but the number was blocked.

"Now what?" I knew it was Julio again by the voice. He really had too much time on his hands.

"You should go to the window."

"Didn't I tell you I'm not playing these games."

"Well, I guess you're not tryna save Naima after all." I stood up quick.

"Go to the window." I ran over in hopes to see her.

"That black van has her inside." I went to the door.

"Tell her mother who's standing directly next to you I'm not playing and if the ring isn't returned, she will regret it." I repeated his statement. She asked for the phone and I don't know what they spoke about but she was cursing him out.

"Fuck this." I ran out the door.

BOOM! The van exploded in front of me. My ears were ringing as I hit the ground, but that screeching scream could be heard miles away.

"NOOOOOO!"

To Be Continued…